SPIRIT CASTER II
THE COSMIC QUEEN
LIFE CUNNINGHAM

ASTRAPÍ
THE KÍTR
PHOENIX ISLAND

THE BLACK CONTINENT
'S DESERT
EBONY
LIVADIA
KARDIA
NOTIO PAGO

CHAPTER ONE
CRYSTAL

"When you both asked me to join you in your fight, my entire life changed. I had my first real battle and went on an adventure that changed the course of history as we know it. I traveled to Phoenix Island to fight the legendary Phoenix, flew across the Kítrinos Desert to save Crystal from an army of bandits, and after all that I was finally put on trial for being one of the most dangerous Shēna alive. Sentenced to death for simply existing even though I'm not even a teenager yet. But with the help of my friends we escaped, took on the Five Armaments and defeated the King of the Black Continent in a battle to the death. And now there's nothing left for us to do except celebrate our victory with an amazing beach vacation."

"Alizeh," Ana cut in while only half paying attention. "We know. We were there."

"I know but how could you guys *not* wanna talk about it?"

"Because I'm unbelievably tired and would rather be home right now. I didn't think your parting words would take so long."

I could tell that wasn't a lie. When she moved her long locks from in front of her face, I could see bags under one of her eyes. I couldn't see the other one since it was covered by a new, thicker eye patch. And her dark, normally glistening skin seemed dryer than usual. This woman was truly exhausted from our travels.

Completely unlike Alizeh who was still bursting with energy. Her big green eyes were wide and her golden skin matched her current emotion. But I guess that made sense. She was only twelve. Compared to Ana being Eighteen and me just being Seventeen, Alizeh was a baby in comparison. But not one to be underestimated.

We stood at a crossroad in the middle of the night. The shorter path was closer to the barn where Alizeh's parents and my sister were staying. The other road led straight to Nótio Págo. This is where it was time to say our goodbyes to Ana.

"I'm pretty sure she's just stalling," I laughed. "It's gonna be a while before the next time we see you again so I can understand why."

"Please," Ana scoffed as she hopped back on her giant wolf, Silver, "We'll meet again in less than a month. It barely warrants a goodbye. You two shouldn't be getting all sentimental *now* of all times. The dangerous part is over. Next time we see each other it'll be all fun and relaxation."

"Yeah, I guess you're right," Alizeh smiled.

Ana raised her hand as Silver began to walk off. "Until we meet again."

I raised my hand right back. "Until then."

And with that, Silver sped off until they were both out of sight. Now it was just Alizeh and I. It would've almost been depressing if we weren't so close to our destination. The thought of seeing our families again put us in pretty high spirits.

"I'm so glad we can finally go home!" Alizeh sang. "Going to war with the King and his forces was fun and all but I'm glad we finally just get to relax for a while."

"All that was fun for you?" I laughed at the absurd claim.

"Of course! The King was *actually* going to kill us. I've never been so close to death before! And that's saying a lot since we all have almost died more than once in the last couple of months."

"I've said it before, and I'll say it again. That mindset of yours will be the death of you."

"Oh, come on Crystal. You can't tell me you didn't have a *little* bit of fun breaking out of his castle and beating the crap out of Kira."

"None of that was fun for me," I explained with a less joyful demeanor. "I don't like fighting, Alizeh. I simply went there to get my revenge and now that it's all over I plan to move on with my life."

Alizeh stopped in place as if something serious just came into her mind. "What does that mean?" She cocked her head slightly looking at me with those big jade eyes. "What do you plan to do with your life now that all of that stuff with the Princess is over?"

Her question came as a shock to me only because I didn't know the answer to it myself. I never thought about how life would be after I got my revenge. Where would Wren and I go? I didn't want to go back home. Seeing it would bring back too many negative memories, not only for me but for Wren too. I wasn't even sure if I wanted to step a single foot back in Nótio Págo.

"I'm not sure," I answered. "Can Wren and I stay with you until I figure it out?"

"You can stay for however long you like. If it was up to me then I'd have you live with us forever," she laughed.

"I wouldn't be too mad at that idea," I smiled.

Alizeh looked around before saying, "Hey, this place is starting to feel pretty familiar."

"What do you mean?"

Before she answered me, she pulled out her Spirit Caster and said, **_"Paírno Ptísi,"_** and without warning, she jumped high into the air leaving only a large gust of wind behind. Moments later she came floating right back down to the ground.

"What was that all about?" I asked.

"We're really close. When I was up there, I could see the barn."

"Really?"

"Yeah, now come on I'll race ya. **_Grígoros Ánemos!_**" she said before speeding off leaving yet another gust of wind.

"Hey, no fair!" I laughed before running after her.

It took me a few minutes, but I finally caught up. She stood by the door as she waited for me and said, "Took you long enough. You ready to go in?"

After I caught my breath I smiled and finally said, "Yeah, I'm ready."

Alizeh slammed the door open and shouted, "We're back!"

Alizeh's words and spirit fizzled out. We were expecting a warm welcome from our loving families but instead we saw something that was so unexpected, we both didn't know how to react.

Alizeh's mother was lying against the wall in a daze and covered in blood. Her father was face down on the floor. I couldn't even tell if he was alive. And my sister, Wren was being grabbed and yanked by the collar by a familiar looking woman with red hair and a nasty scar that seared half of her face. Even though the scar made her look different, I could still recognize her. It was Arachne. A member of the Five Armaments. The same one who poisoned us, allowing the late King to imprison us.

Wren saw me first before Arachne did and shouted, "Crystal!" looking relieved at my arrival.

Arachne was equally as surprised as she uttered a single word under her breath. "Shit."

Alizeh's eyes darted around the room before landing right on Arachne. She raised her fist with the intent of attacking with a powerful spell but before she could pull it off, Arachne yanked Wren close and pointed her dagger at my sister's neck.

"Wait!" I stopped Alizeh, grabbing her trembling wrist so she wouldn't hit Wren. Then I looked to Arachne, commanding her to, "Let my sister go."

"Can't do that," she shook her head. "I'm gonna get out of here now. And I'm taking these two with me," she gestured her dagger down at Alizeh's father, Tal. "If you follow me, then I'll slit their throats."

Alizeh took a step towards her, while saying, "If you think you're leaving here alive then you've gone insane."

That threat was unlike her. But she herself was being faced with a threat towards her family so it wasn't exactly surprising.

Arachne quickly pulled her dagger back up to Wren's throat and this time she drew blood. This wasn't the first time she had gotten a blade held to her throat. But this was the first time the blade was held by someone who wouldn't hesitate to kill her.

I quickly grabbed Alizeh by the arm so she couldn't take another step. She was tense. As if she herself was using every ounce of her will to stop herself from killing this woman.

"What is it you want?" I asked Arachne. "Are you just looking for revenge after what happened in Ebony? Did Kira put you up to this?"

Arachne snorted at the accusation. "As if Kira ever had the spine to do what needed to be done. Your pointless little war means nothing to me and Ebony could burn for all I care."

"Then what the hell are you after?" Alizeh seethed, unamused by the pointless stalling.

Arachne smirked at her and relaxed for a moment before answering. "Godhood." And then she tensed back up and as loud as she could she shouted, "Thelonious!"

The earth shook beneath us as something, or rather *someone* sprung from the dirt in-between the both of us.

"Ekrígnymai!" they shouted.

Steam erupted from beneath us, causing an explosion to force us through the barn wall and outside into the open field.

I tumbled onto my back but quickly got back to my feet.

"Alizeh, you ok?" I shouted.

She was hovering a foot above the grass. She never let her body hit the floor and she didn't have a scratch on her. Her instincts had been on fight or flight mode ever since she saw her family in danger.

"Yeah, I'm fine," she told me while not taking her eyes off the barn.

"What the hell was that?" I asked. "The attack came so fast; I almost didn't have time to shield my body with Rēa."

"It's another Shēna," she answered as the cloaked man walked out of the barn and through the steam towards us. His calm and collected demeanor was almost unsettling. But not as unsettling as what he was holding in his right hand. It was an *Evolved Spirit Caster*. I had only met two others who possessed such a powerful wand. I've held it at one point, but I couldn't handle its full power. I doubted this man held the same restrictions.

The man removed his hood to get a better look at us and in turn we got a better look at him. He had short, wavy, brown curls and intense green eyes. His skin was slightly darker than mine but much lighter than Alizeh's.

"There's an immense amount of power surging through him," Alizeh continued. "But he doesn't look familiar."

"I guess it doesn't matter. Regardless, my sister and your parents are still in the barn and in harm's way. And this guy's our only obstacle. Do you think you're fast enough to get past him?

"I'll have to be. Take him on while I go after Arachne."

And without any hesitation, she launched herself towards him but he was ready for her. Before she could pass him up, he dragged his staff across the dirt and swung, forcing a plethora of sharpened stone pillars to explode from the ground and shoot back in our direction. Alizeh went to a screeching halt and leaped back to avoid the widespread attack that seemed to have no end in sight.

Soon the pillars wrapped like a jungle, eating Alizeh into the brush while quickly making its way towards me. There was no way that I was fast enough to run away from it. So I had to go through it. I ran and jumped over the first pillar and slid under the next one. It was like trying to maneuver around an army of giant coiled snakes.

But it became more and more overwhelming as the amalgamation of dirt and stone rose into the air, lifting us along with it. I was getting too slow. Too unbalanced. Until I finally slipped and tumbled down, unable to stop myself from the eminent jagged stone that was in my path.

Before my body was torn apart I felt something pull on my wrist and raise me high into the air. It was Alizeh flying us up while narrowly avoiding all the attacks that came our way.

Until suddenly, everything stopped. What once felt like a hive mind of animate monsters and beasts given life to kill us soon turned into a twisted lifeless mountain of dirt that slowly started to crumble away.

"Where'd he go?" Alizeh asked while turning us in every direction. I looked around with her, not being able to see anything from the dust clouds that scattered from the spell.

"Take us down, *now*." I ordered, realizing our families were still in danger.

She quickly lowered us to the ground and as soon as our feet hit the dirt, we both darted into the destroyed barn.

"They're gone!" Alizeh panicked.

It wasn't just Arachne and her mysterious ally. Wren was gone along with Alizeh's father.

"Damnit," I cursed under my breath. "That attack was all just one big distraction!"

"Alizeh," her mother called in a daze, snatching our attention. She was sitting against the wall, covered in blood.

"Mom?" Alizeh called as she quickly went by her side to hold her hands. We both looked down to see the nasty wounds. Both of her wrists were slit. And not only that, The wounds themselves were dark; purple veins stretched out from the sliced flesh. "Mom, are you ok?" Alizeh looked back into her baggy eyes.

But her mother didn't answer as her glossy eyes started to shut down and her body went limp.

"We have to get her to a doctor, *now*!" Alizeh shouted.

***

I stayed outside the barn, pacing back and forth whilst waiting for Alizeh to come back. As soon as she realized the true danger her mother was in, she rushed outside and blasted off into the sky to get her to the closest hospital. I had no idea how long it had been since I last saw her, but it felt like hours had passed.

As I waited, something fell from the sky and created an explosion of dust causing me to jump back. Once the dust cleared, I saw Alizeh there with a grim look on her face.

"Alizeh?" I spoke. "You're back. What happened to your mother? Is she ok?"

"She's alive ... for now. The doctor thinks she's been poisoned and they're not sure how long she has. It could be anywhere between weeks or even just days."

"Alizeh ... I'm sorry," I looked down, not being able to bare looking her in the eyes. I was still coming to grips with the loss of my own parents and could only imagine how someone her age could be reacting to the news.

"Don't be," she reassured me. "There's a chance she'll survive if I act quickly."

"What do we have to do?"

"The doctor said that the only way she has a chance of surviving is if he can make a special medicine to combat the poison. The only problem with that is the one herb he needs to complete it is only located in *The Kitrinos Desert*."

"Alright then, I'll come with you. We can get it together and come back as quickly as possible. After that we can find Wren and your dad."

"No."

"What do you mean *no*?" I asked. There was a certain way it slipped out of her mouth that scared me. I'd never seen her so serious before.

"Crystal, you need to focus on finding Dad and Wren. We have no idea why they were taken. So we don't know how much time they have either."

"Alright then I'm going back to Ebony."

"Why Ebony?"

"Because she's a part of the Five Armaments. That means Kira should know where she is. I'm going to question her about it. When you're done with finding the plant then you should come find me there."

"Sounds like a plan. We'll leave at dawn."

CHAPTER TWO
FLINT

I floated atop the thick warm layer of lava as if it was water. It didn't burn. If anything, its warmth was actually quite comforting. It was only canceled out by my mother's cold spirit.

"Do you remember what happened? Why you're here?" she asked while standing atop the lava and looking down at me.

"I remember fighting the King," I answered. "Did I die? It kinda feels like I died. Is this Hell?"

"No, Flint," she shook her head. "You didn't die. But you should've."

I took a deep breath and said flatly, "Yeah, I know."

"You know there will be a cost, don't you?"

"What do you care?" I scoffed while looking away from her.

She took a moment to respond. "More than I let on, I suppose." I looked back at her to see that she wasn't looking at me. Her eyes were low, almost melancholic. She finally glanced back at me and continued, "Flint. I can feel that your Rēa is draining. Once it's gone, I don't think I'll ever be able to communicate with you like this again."

"So basically, nothing will change," I half joked.

"Flint ..." she crouched down and placed her hand on my arm to make sure I was hearing what she was saying. She needed me to pay attention to her next words. But before she could say another word it was over.

I shot up from my slumber and looked around in a cold sweat. I was in a bedroom that wasn't my own. The last thing I remembered was that I was holding down the King. Then Rai hit us with their lightning. I used every ounce of Rēa in my body to block the attack. Maybe even more than I had to spare. While I was in mid thought the door opened and Rai was the only one to come through it.

"Flint," they stopped looking fairly shocked, but only for a moment, "you're awake! Took you long enough."

Their face was always hard to read. Not just emotionally but even on a physical level. The first time we met I thought they were a girl. But when I referred to them as such ... well let's just say they didn't mesh well with the title. Or any title for that matter. I didn't get it but to each their own.

I probably wasn't certain of their gender because of their young face. They were just a few years younger than me and a few years older than Alizeh. So they were still probably growing into it.

"Rai," I asked, "what happened? Where are we?"

"We're at an Inn not too far away from Ebony," Rai answered as they walked over to the bed and sat down beside me with a loaf of bread in their hand. They ripped it in half and handed me a piece. "Here, eat this. You must be starving."

I took it and asked, "Where is everyone? And what happened to the King? Did we win?"

"Yeah, we won," they smiled. "The King's dead."

"And Ana?"

"Don't worry, your girlfriend's fine. She, Crystal and Alizeh went home a few days ago. But, they promised to come back here three weeks from now to see us again."

There was solace to be taken in that. I wanted to see Ana so badly while I was here, but it seemed that I'd have to wait a little bit longer.

"How long have I been out for?" I asked.

"A week."

No wonder I felt completely drained. It took everything I had to survive. And in that moment I didn't feel a spec of Rēa in me.

I finally took a bite of the dry bread before Rai told me, "Now that you're awake there's no need for me to stick around this place anymore."

"Where are you going?" I asked.

"Back to Ebony."

I stopped myself mid bite to look back up at them, "Wait, why?"

"Because my grandmother's still there."

"So what are you planning to do? Bust her out? You know that's not just a simple task. Ebony's probably on high alert after what we just did. It's gonna be another huge battle if you go."

"Actually, I don't think it will be as complicated as you think."

"And why's that?"

"Because there's something about the Princess that's ... *different*. I don't know how to explain it, but I think she's changed."

"Changed how?"

"Well while you were unconscious, and after we beat The King, she just let us go," they shrugged.

"So what? You think that just because she didn't wanna fight after all hell broke loose, it means she's on our side now?"

"I know it sounds crazy—"

"And naive," I interrupted.

"But ... I don't know. I'm still going to talk to her. I'm going to ask her to release my grandmother."

"And what will you do if she says no?"

"Then I'll fight through Kira and her army until I free her."

I pondered on the thought of Rai fighting the uphill battle in order to get what they wanted and wondered if it was just in a Shēna's blood to try and do the impossible.

I finished my last bite of bread and said, "Ok, I'm coming with you."

"No, I don't want to drag anyone else into this."

"It's fine. I was planning on going back to Ebony anyways."

"What do *you* need to go back for?" they asked.

"The Black Continent's army invaded Phoenix Island. If Kira has turned over a new leaf, then there's a chance I can persuade her to get her knights off my homeland. I also need to make sure that all the men I came here with are alright."

"And if she says no?"

"Then I guess we both have a fight on our hands."

Rai smiled and asked, "Can you stand?"

"I think so."

"Then get yourself ready. We're heading to Ebony."

CHAPTER THREE
ALIZEH

I had a restless night. Don't get me wrong, I *needed* the break after traveling for so long but I couldn't get over the fact that my mother was waiting on me to save her. She was suffering and I was the only person who could stop it.

As soon as the sun peeked over the horizon, I jumped out of bed and started packing all the essentials.

"You're up early," I heard Crystal say without a shred of grogginess in her voice. I looked over at her still laying on the other side of the barn with heavy bags under her eyes.

"I never fell asleep," I told her. "But I'm guessing you already knew that."

"I figured," she told me while standing from off the floor. "Are you sure you're ready to go out there on your own?"

"No. I'm not sure. But I guess this is a good time to find out."

"Yeah," she sighed, "I guess it is."

As I finished strapping my goggles to my head, I turned back around to see her heavy eyes as she put on her gloves, almost looking past her hands, or beyond even the floor.

"What's wrong?" I asked.

She took another deep breath before answering and refused to look at me. "It's just, I don't know when I'm going to see you again. Or even *if* I'll see you again," her voice started to tremble. "And this time Ana won't be here to help us. Potentially we're both heading into a lot of danger."

"Well, *everything* we've ever done together has been dangerous."

"I know, but even then, we've always done it together," she finally looked me in my eyes. "You're one of my first true friends. And not being able to do this with you by my side ... and not knowing if your safe—"

I've never seen Crystal in such a state. I had only known her for a few months but within that time we've gotten close, going through hell and back with each other. And within that time I've never seen her break. She led the charge on The King and she's the reason I was able to go on this adventure in the first place. And because of that I was in debt to her. I couldn't bear to see the same woman he brought me so much happiness on the verge of tears.

"Don't talk like that," I cut her off. "We *have* to make it out safely. It's not just about revenge. This time it's about saving the ones closest to us. And I have faith in the both of us. We'll do this and come back alive. And then we'll all go to the beach just like we planned."

Crystal shed a few silent tears before I walked over to her and gave her a big hug. She bent down and hugged me so tightly. Tighter than she's ever done before.

She let go and wiped away her tears while saying, "Ok Alizeh, just make sure you come straight to Ebony after helping your mother."

"Don't worry Crystal. I will," I smiled, while backing away from her. This wasn't going to be some grand adventure like last time. All I needed to do was get the plant and come back. It was more akin to a daily chore if anything. "I'm going now."

"Alright, be safe," she waved.

"Right back at you," I said before running outside, pulling out my Spirit Caster and yelling, ***"Paírno Ptísi!"*** I blasted off into the sky with my sights set on Kítrinos.

***

Once I flew over the sandy border, all the memories from this country came flooding in. The last time I was in Kítrinos marked the first time I ever felt true fear. All I could think about was Barin, the man who had kidnapped Crystal and came so close to killing Ana and I. My hope was that since I was traveling by air, I wouldn't have to have another run in with someone like him.

I put more Rēa into my spell to test my limits. A white ring formed around me as I went faster than I ever thought I could. Separating from Crystal was actually a good thing. No one else was around to slow me down. It was exhilarating!

But the fun was short-lived. I could already see my destination coming over the horizon. I stopped myself in mid air and as soon as I did, a loud boom exploded from my mere presence after flying faster than sound.

I descended down into what looked like paradise. It was an oasis. The only part of the desert that had life: from lush plants and tall trees to lively animals and buzzing insects. A small mountain wrapped halfway around the small oasis and from it spewed a white waterfall that landed into a crystal clear lake.

I was looking for the water fýkia. A special type of seaweed that only grew in Kítrinos. But it can't grow or survive in extreme heat so actually finding it in this desert was extremely rare. You'd specifically have to look for an oasis just like the one I was standing in to find it. More specifically you'd have to find it in the water.

I put down my bag and tossed my Spirit Caster into the sand. Afterwards I changed my clothes and took a jar out of my bag to have something to put the seaweed in. After readying myself, I dove into the water to search for the plant.

I searched in the lake past sunset, constantly needing to swim back up for air since there was such a wide area to search. But I wasn't stopping until I found it.

Eventually I finally spotted it. A single small patch of water fýkia. I quickly grabbed it, put it all into the jar, and went back up to the surface.

Coming up for my last breath of air was relieving. I looked up into the black sky to see that the stars were out. It looked like It took longer than I thought It would to find the plant. But the hardest part was over. Now I just needed to bring it back to my mother.

"What are you doing in our Oasis?" A voice asked from behind me. I turned around as I was still in the water and saw the last thing I wanted to deal with. A large group of bandits surrounded my stuff. And in front of them all was a man I hoped I would never see again.

His golden eyes almost glowed in the dark like a wild animal as he stared me down. His dark skin shined under the moonlight. He held my Spirit Caster in his hand with a smirk on his face.

"Alizeh Green," Barin called with a joyous tone. "It's good to see you again. Let's have a chat." His tone then shifted into something more serious. "But first get out of the water." I had to listen. With my Spirit Caster now in his hands, I was completely defenseless.

I slowly walked out of the spring, shivering from the cold winds that the desert nights produced. Once I was in front of him, I asked, "Can I at least go to my bag to put my normal clothes back on?"

"Sorry, no can do," he answered. "I'm not leaving you with anything that can help you escape." He looked down at the jar that was in my hands and asked, "What is that?"

"It's just water fýkia," I answered hesitantly.

"You found that in the lake didn't you? This is our territory which means that's our property," he said as he snatched the jar away from me. "I hear this stuff has some worth to those willing to pay. I'm sure I can sell it for a decent price."

My heart sank as he tore away the only thing that could save my mother. "Wait no! I need that! My mother's sick and—"

"I don't care," he interrupted as he tossed the jar over to one of his men. "Tie her up by the wrists. We're taking her with us."

***

After a lot of walking throughout the sandy dunes we made it far enough to the point where the oasis was out of sight. I was surrounded by his goons as they all pulled camels along our path. Both my wrists were bound by a long rope that Barin had the other end of, giving me no room to escape. I could have easily ripped the rope and gotten myself unbound if I had my Spirit Caster but without it I was too weak to break away.

It was silent for a while until he finally decided to ask me an unexpected question. "How's Crystal doing?"

"What?" I asked, too surprised that he would even ask about her at a time like this.

"Is Crystal still alive?"

"What's that matter to you?" The thought of him actually caring for her well-being was a baffling one. He was a killer. At least that's all I saw him as. Just like Ana, he lived for battle. The only difference was that he fought for himself. Although, the way Crystal described him was something totally different. After Crystal escaped from him she told Ana and I that he saved her from his own men. Other bandits who worked under him planned on torturing her, or worse. He killed every last one of them. Although he claimed to do it simply so that his *'merchandise'* wouldn't get damaged. Cristal didn't talk about much else when it came to being his captive, but when she spoke his name there was always a sense of sadness and maybe even disappointment in her eyes.

"Just answer the damn question," he groaned.

I paused for a moment before saying, "Yeah, she's fine."

"That's a relief. I heard about the battle that took place in Ebony and figured it was you guys. If you're both still alive then that means you pulled it off. If you survive this then I want you to tell Crystal I'm proud of her."

'If' I survive this? It was a strange shift. A moment of compassion for Crystal followed by an ominous threat towards me. I still didn't understand his motives.

"What do you plan on doing to me?" I finally asked.

"I plan on settling the score with you," he answered without looking at me.

"What score? I don't recall doing anything to you! If anything *I* should be settling the score with *you*!"

"For what exactly?"

"*For what?*" I boiled. "You stole all of the gold that we collected, you tried to sell Crystal as a slave, *and* you tried to kill me and Ana!"

"I only did all that stuff for the money. Morpheus paid us all handsomely for the job. And besides, you're here now which means whatever he was scheming didn't work. So no harm no foul."

"You're insane! You can't possibly think that actually justifies your actions?"

"Stop yelling, we're right next to each other and it's giving me a headache."

I wanted to shout at him some more but I got my composure back and asked him once more, "What score are you trying to settle?"

He then stopped and turned around to face me before lifting his shirt up to show his chest. A giant twisted and mangled scar took up most of his abdomen. It was in the same spot that I pierced him in during our battle. It was amazing to see that he actually survived such a wound.

"This is the score I want to settle," he answered. "You gave me this wound with the intention to kill, but you left without finishing the job."

"So what are you going to do? Kill me to get revenge?"

"Yes. But not like this. I want to fight you at full strength. I'm going to give you back your Spirit Caster. And once I do, *that's* when we'll have a battle to settle things. A true battle to the death."

This wasn't my first battle to the death so the thought of it didn't terrify me. But it did make me incredibly uneasy. I've fought Barin before. He was strong. And he would've killed me if Ana wasn't there to save me. Technically the Rēa in my blood and the destructive spells in my repertoire made me stronger than him but there was something about the way he fought. His reaction time, speed and strength. He wasted no energy in any of his attacks. Even after Ana beat him she claimed that he was still stronger than her.

"I understand you wanting to fight me. And even wanting to hurt me. But I don't understand why you would want to put your own life on the line for that."

"It's just something that a Zubarian like myself was made for. Killing and putting my life on the line for that goal. Especially when it comes to you Shēna."

"Do you have a problem with my race?" I asked with scrunched brows.

"Not exactly. But our races were once at odds were they not? It just feels right for this to be our final battle."

His point was almost valid. Long ago some ruler in the Royal bloodline put our two races at odds. And our race fueled by magic was forced to destroy their race of warriors. A fact that I had only learned recently from meeting Ana.

"Our race's don't *have* to be at odds," I argued. "Just look at Ana. She's a Zubarian just like you and she's one of my best friends in the whole wide world. And besides, that war that happened between our races happened a long time ago."

Barin's eyes turned red just like they did in his battle with Ana as he activated his Warriors Spirit. He yanked my rope pulling me closer to him and put his face right in front of mine to get his point across.

"A long time ago huh? You might be right about that but you seem to be naive towards what that war led to. My race's *extinction*. We were once a proud and powerful race but now look at us. I've only ever met two other Zubarians in my life and one of them was a slave just like me. My race is at the bottom of the barrel in this world and when it comes to the hierarchy on this continent we're lucky to rival literal *maggots*. I've suffered my entire life because of what I am. The fact that you're right about that damn war being so long ago is what pisses me off. For an event to happen before I was even born while still having such a profound affect on my existence ... It makes me furious!"

He grabbed me by the neck and lifted me into the air. This situation was all too familiar. The only difference was that he was actually angry. There was no telling if he would hold himself back and this time Ana and Crystal weren't here to save me. I honestly think he would've snapped my neck from how tight he was squeezing if he hadn't gotten distracted from one of his men shouting from behind him.

It was a scream of terror and pain. We all looked to where the cry came from and saw one of the bandits gushing blood from their chest. They were impaled by something.

The man started to rise in the air and the spot of sand that he was standing on started to shuffle and swell as if something was stirring from underneath.

Finally, a monstrous beast with eight legs, giant pincher claws, and black armor all over its body emerged from the sand. It held the bandit's limp body with its tail as it pierced through his chest. It looked like a giant scorpion.

"What is that thing?" I choked.

Barin didn't answer. He simply dropped me into the sand and immediately ran past one of the camels, taking a spear from off its back, while sprinting full speed towards the scorpion. He threw the spear and I watched as it flew through the air and pierced the scorpion right in its eye.

The scorpion shook in pain and charged at Barin but as soon as it got close, he jumped high into the air and right on the scorpion's back, taking the spear, and pushing it deeper into its head until the monster finally collapsed.

"Is everyone ok?" he asked as he stepped off the dying beast. "If so, then let's get a move on. We shouldn't stay in this area for too much longer. We don't know what else is out here."

Right after he said that, multiple explosions of sand started to fly everywhere. More scorpions started to dig their way up and before we knew it we were surrounded. Everyone pulled out their own weapons but I had nothing. Without any warning, the scorpions attacked and the bandits attacked back. Before I knew it there were weapons and pools of blood spilling everywhere. The sand in the air mixed with the low amount of moonlight made it hard to see anything.

I ran for my life, evading as many monsters as possible. Jumping over and under their attacks making sure that their tails didn't hit me. But there was only so much I could do with my hands tied.

As I ran through the crowd a man fell to the sand and from his body came a large jar filled with water. It was *my* jar! If I could just grab it then I'd be able to get out of here and wouldn't have to worry about any of this. Unfortunately things couldn't have been that easy.

I was just inches away from the jar but before I could pick it up, the leg of a scorpion came crashing down right in front of me and right onto the jar, shattering it and crushing the plant.

The one thing I needed to save my mother was now gone. And the monster in front of me didn't look like it would be so kind as to spare my life so I could go and get another. It looked like my time was up.

The scorpion launched its tail at me to deliver the finishing blow but before it could stab me Barin got in the way and sliced its tail clean off with his sword. He then grabbed me and ran.

"Give me my Spirit Caster!" I shouted.

"No, you'll just escape if I do. I can handle this on my—"

His arrogance was cut short at once, as a scorpion hit us with its claws forcing us to fly back into the sand.

"This isn't a debate! You can't survive without my help!" I yelled as I tried to get back to my feet.

"No," he said while trying to catch his breath after the last attack.

Before we both knew it, scorpions surrounded the two of us in every direction. Barin was still on his knees and I was powerless. There was no way out.

"Barin, give me the wand! I can't afford to die here!" I cried. "*We* can't afford to die here! How are you going to fight me if we're both dead?"

His eyes widened as their tails and claws darted towards us. He reached into the inside of his shirt and chucked my Spirit Caster towards me. As soon as I grabbed it I broke through the rope and shouted, ***"Tyfónas!"***

The intense wind swirled in every direction making a sand storm picking up everyone and everything around me. Being reunited with my Spirit Caster gave me rejuvenated power. I felt more powerful than I had ever felt before. I looked down at my Spirit Caster and saw that it was longer, like a staph. It evolved! I couldn't revel in it because I was completely livid.

I came all this way just to end up empty handed. Because of Barin, and these monsters, so much of my time was wasted! I felt like destroying everything! So I decided that was exactly what I was going to do.

I poured all of my Rēa into my Spirit Caster and the power of my spell went to its zenith. The winds were so powerful that they started to rip the monsters apart. Their limbs were torn off one by one as they all went flying in the air. And they weren't the only ones that were getting punished. The same happened to the bandits. They flew into the air getting sucked up in my spell and their bodies were being torn apart from the extreme winds as well. Blood spiraled around me and all I could see was red.

The thing that made me even more angry was the fact that killing everything didn't make me feel better. It wasn't satisfying enough so I released the spell. Sand fell from the sky along with severed limbs and droplets of blood. The blood spilled all over the sand

and my body like rain. Bathing in the blood of my enemies was a bittersweet feeling. They all got what they deserved but was it enough? I wasn't satisfied. I should've inflicted more pain onto them since they were all practically to blame for the soon to be death of my mother.

I heard a thud behind me and once I looked back I saw Barin laying in the sand while covered in his own blood. His eyes opened and he quickly sat up while giving me a deadly glare.

"What the hell *are* you?" I asked. "You shouldn't have survived that."

"You need to stop underestimating me," he smirked. "Sorry to disappoint you but I'm still kicking."

"Don't apologize. I'm glad that you're still alive. I'm not having a good day so I need to let off some steam. You'll be the perfect object for me to let my anger out on."

I released all of my energy out causing wind to spiral around me. A misty aura emanated out of my body as the overwhelming amount of Rēa boiled in my blood. I was going to destroy this man. But not before taking my time. The look in his eyes went from a cold and condescending glare to one of terror. He knew that his time was up and I reveled in that fact. But right after only taking a single step my Spirit Caster shattered and reformed back into its original form. The aura around my body dispersed and the wind stopped completely.

It looked like my Spirit Caster's evolution was a fluke just like Crystal's. A momentary boost in power made simply from my emotions. And now I felt completely drained.

I fell to my knees and almost immediately passed out. The last thing I saw before slipping away was Barin getting up and making his way towards me. I was once again completely defenseless and my fate was up in the air. All I could do was hope he would be more merciful than I. Or at least give me a quick death.

CHAPTER FOUR
ANA

Silver ran full speed through the snowy tundra, not because I told him to, but because he wanted to. He knew exactly where we were and his excitement met no bounds. We were finally home. It felt good to be back in Nótio Págo.

Finally gazing at the temple after all this time was like looking at a bed after a long day of hunting. Once we got to the bridge I hopped off Silver and he collapsed into the snow, rolling around with excitement before quickly burning himself out. I reached into my bag and threw him a raw piece of fish, leaving him to his well earned meal before going across the bridge and back into the temple.

Once I was in the temple, I walked past two men who were working together to carry supplies, and as soon as they spotted me they dropped everything to the floor. One of the men practically gawked at me while the other called my name in disbelief.

I stopped and asked, "Do you two need help with that?"

"N-no!" the man denied. "It's just... I mean," he couldn't find the right words to say.

"Are you ok?" The other man finally asked.

"Yeah, I'm feeling pretty good," I answered before turning the other way. "Thanks for asking."

As I made my way further through the hall I passed by someone else. A really good friend of mine. Cara, a young Zubarian that I was tasked to train. She wasn't as strong as I was, but she was still a great warrior in my eyes.

"Hey Cara," I greeted as I passed by her.

"Hi Ana," she said back before catching herself and doubling back at my mere presence. "Ana? You're alive?" she gasped.

"Apparently," I answered without stopping.

She followed close behind and added, "But you've been gone for months!"

"Only a couple."

"Where'd you go? What happened to your eye?"

These questions didn't seem that important to me so instead I changed the conversation to something that did, "Where's my mother?"

"I believe she's in the meditation chamber. She's been in there a lot since you left. I actually rarely see her anymore."

"I hope I didn't make her worry."

"You made us *all* worry."

I finally stopped walking and said, "Yeah, I'm sorry about that."

"I'm not the one you need to be apologizing to right now."

"Right. I'll explain everything to you later. Right now, I've gotta go see my mother."

I walked away from Cara and went straight to the meditation chamber, taking a deep breath before slowly opening the door. My mother was sitting in the center of the room, still meditating with her eyes completely shut.

"Sit," she said before I could even make a sound.

I listened, closing the door behind me and quickly sat on the soft pillow in front of her. She finally opened her eyes with a stern look that I haven't seen from her since I was a young child. It still terrified me to this day.

"Two months," she finally spoke. "You were gone for *two months* without saying goodbye or even where you were going."

"In my defense, I thought I was going to be out for like an hour, tops."

She reached for my face, caressing it along with the scar that stretched through my eye. She studied my body. Every scar. Every blood stained bandage. There were too many gaps that she couldn't possibly fill in herself.

"Tell me everything."

***

She took a pause before saying, "That was a lot more than I expected."

"*You're* telling *me*?"

"How do you feel?"

"Tired," I started to get up to my feet. "And hungry."

"Is that all?"

I stopped to think before answering, "I feel accomplished. Like I really made a difference."

"Do you have any regrets?"

"Besides getting my ass handed to me a few times? No. I'd do it all again in a heartbeat."

"I've always loved that conviction of yours Ana. If your father was here, he'd be more than proud of what you've accomplished."

"He *was* there with me. I felt him. I *saw* him. He helped me every step of the way."

"Well I'm glad you already know. Now go eat and get some rest."

I did a quick bow and left the room, shutting the door behind me. Cara was leaning against the wall standing right next to the door, obviously listening in on the conversation.

"What did you hear?" I asked.

"What makes you think I was listening?"

"Because you're always listening."

"What can I say? I don't like being left in the dark."

I rolled my good eye and made my way to the cafeteria. She followed close behind and said, "I heard *some* things, not all. So I still have a few questions."

"Shoot."

"Did you say you fought a Phoenix or did I hear you wrong?"

"You heard right."

"Sweet. Ok next question. You and the hero of Phoenix Island; I think you said his name was Flint, right? Did you guys—"

"No."

"You didn't even let me finish."

"Because I already know what you're gonna ask. He's definitely my type. Handsome. Powerful. The potential to lead," as I spoke I thought about the time he saved the entire island from sure destruction. I was the only one who witnessed his pure determination and power. "But," I continued, "that boy has a lot of growing to do."

"Well if you don't want him then maybe you should introduce him to me some time."

I glared at her with a raised eyebrow forcing her to immediately raise her hands up and say, "Just kidding! I know not to go after your own *personal* prey. Ok last question. What the hell is a *Warrior's Spirit*?"

I stopped and gave her a grin before unleashing the ability right before her. She took a step, startled by my one red eye and shredded physique. But I was too tired to sustain it so I almost immediately dropped out of it and returned to my normal form while still struggling to stand.

"Ana, what *was* that just now?" she asked.

I turned around and continued walking before saying, "It's the next thing I'm going to teach you."

***

I tore through the bear meat, as if I were the predator who hunted it, causing Cara to grimace as if she herself were witnessing a mauling.

"When's the last time you ate?" Cara winced.

"Yesterday. But the last time I had a *real* meal was probably back on Phoenix Island. Flint's a surprisingly good cook," I told her while tossing the bone towards Silver.

"He cooked for you?" she squinted with a coy smile. "Like, breakfast?"

"He cooked for *everyone*," I rolled my eyes.

"*Right*," she rolled her eyes right back before changing her focus. "So, tell me more about this *Warrior's spirit*."

Once she asked, I finished slurping down the rest of my steaming soup and slammed it down to the table to get rid of all distractions.

"It's a whole nother level of power. Like a state of being that doubles—no. *Triples* your power. It's overwhelming and I completely lost my sense of self the first time I activated it."

"So that's the power that your mother told us about?" she leaned in closer over the table. "A Zubarian's peak?"

"Peak?" I leaned back in my chair and looked up at the ceiling, pondering the word. "No," I corrected. "It's not like that. This felt like the beginning of my power. I know I can get a lot stronger."

I thought about how strong Barin was after he kidnapped Crystal. If he wasn't already injured prior to our battle when he fought Alizeh then there was a chance that I wouldn't have beaten him even *with* my Warrior's Spirit. And I had absolutely no chance against Ranne. It's a miracle that I'm still alive to tell the tale of these two battles.

"But the only way I can do that," I continued, "is by having someone who's strong enough to give me a challenge and push me farther than ever before. You're the only person with the potential to do that. But not as you currently are."

"So that's the reason why you need me to achieve that state? To make you even stronger than you already are?" she asked while leaning back in her seat.

I cocked my head, "You say that as if I'm already the strongest."

"You're stronger than most men will ever be."

"Cara, if there's anything that I've learned from my journey," I started to tell her while leaning in close to pull up my eye patch. She looked almost startled but couldn't take her two *good* eyes off of my one *mutilated* eye and continued saying, "it's that there's always a bigger fish."

Cara shook off that disturbed look on her face, finally understanding what I was getting at and asked, "Alright, so where do we start?"

I slipped my eye patch back over the dead eye and leaned back, making the conversation go back to its casual roots.

"Tell me Cara," I started to ask, "have you ever been in a *real* fight before?"

"What do you mean?"

"Have you ever been on the brink of death with only your Zubarian blood and instincts to guide you?"

She pondered for a bit before answering, "Well there was that one time when we went hunting and that bear attacked us. Thought we were gonna die until you scared it off."

I put my hand on my chin and looked off trying to recall the moment.

"No," I told her. "That wouldn't be enough."

"What do you mean?"

"I was there to protect you like a safety net. You weren't desperate enough to use your own power to save yourself."

"So the only way to unlock that power is to be in a truly life threatening situation? Sounds like achieving such a thing is out of my hands."

"Yeah it would be out of your hands wouldn't it?" I agreed while still pondering the thought. "But it wouldn't be out of mine."

Cara tilted her head and straightened her brows while asking, "What exactly do you mean by that?"

I looked back at her, dead in her eyes and answered, "I mean that if I really wanted to, then I could put you in that situation, and you probably wouldn't be able to stop me."

Cara looked tense. Like she was dreading what I was about to say next. But she didn't stop me. So I continued on.

"Cara, why don't you and I have a little battle to the death?"

CHAPTER FIVE
ANA

"Absolutely not," my mother answered dismissively towards my proposal while lighting her candles.

"Come on mom," I begged, "it's the only way we're going to unlock her potential."

"By killing each other?" she turned back as if I were speaking in a different language.

"We won't end up killing each other as long as she taps into her new power. Once she does that, then you can stop the match right then and there."

She dropped her burning sage down in its tray and turned back towards me finally giving us her full attention.

"Wait, are you actually serious?"

"Of course I'm serious! All she needs is a little *push*," I said while walking back and forth thinking of what it would take. "We'll have to fight with weapons. And the fight can't stop until she achieves the form."

My mother looked at Cara and asked, "You're actually ok with putting your life on the line?"

"Oh," she was caught off guard by the question and grabbed the back of her neck while avoiding eye contact with my mother. "Well I don't actually know. If Ana thinks it'll work—"

"Which it will," I cut in.

"*Right,*" she continued. "Then I'm willing to give it a try."

"*See?*" I gestured thinking that it would be all the approval we needed, but my mother just sat there, glaring at me. "Come on," I sighed, "Isn't it like, tradition or something for us to have battles like this to test our worth?"

"Tradition?" she scoffed. "Yes it's traditional, but it's also archaic."

"I would've never figured you of all people would scoff at tradition," I argued.

She continued to glare at me but this time in a more softer and understanding manner. I was getting to her.

"You can stop the battle as soon as Cara unlocks the form," I reminded. "No one has to die."

"Fine," she finally gave in. "You can both have your little battle but I'll be watching over you and if I think for a second that either one of you can't handle it, I'm putting a stop to it."

"Fine by me," I shrugged knowing that was the best I was going to get.

I looked over at Cara to see her response but she didn't have one. She was completely silent. So silent to the point where it was unnerving. It made me wonder if all this was really a good idea.

No. There wasn't any room for doubt. She can handle the challenge. I believe in her. Because she's my only chance of becoming stronger.

***

Everyone in the temple was gathered in an underground arena that hadn't been used since I was a child. The chamber's stone walls were carved out and had murals of soldiers long gone etched into them. The once smooth floor had dozens of scratches and chips from the bladed weapons and blunt objects worn into it over the years. Light maroon stains of blood were left to fill them. The only thing to light the room were torches scattered about and a rather large fire pit that was elevated onto a small stage that my mother was standing on.

Normally everyone watching would be cheering or grinning ear to ear but today they were all silent creating quite the somber atmosphere. I would've completely hated it if not for the few men and women, beating on their drums to add music to the event. My mother stood in front of a pelt, covered in swords, spears, daggers and whatever other weapon she could think of. They were all there.

"You may both use any single weapon of your choosing," my mother explained.

Cara squatted down and glanced at the pallet, hovering her hand over each of them, hesitant to pick any one of them up. *I* wasn't so indecisive. With a whistle I called for Silver and he quickly came with my sword and scabbard hooked on to his saddle.

It was a weapon that was gifted to me during the battle of Ebony. A golden sword made of pure *Chrysó-Pyk*, the densest metal in the world. It seemed a bit unfair to use such a weapon against Cara but this wasn't any normal spar. This was a battle to the death. A battle that would take all the experience and training we had in our lives to put into one moment. I earned this sword.

As I unhooked it, I asked my mother, "You said any weapon of our choosing, right?"

She simply nodded.

Cara looked back down, realizing that we were now waiting on her, and quickly picked up a battle ax. A weapon she had only just started to get the hang of. Not the worst option but definitely not her best. But she was still inexperienced. It's hard to say what her best actually was.

Two men came to pick up the pelt of weapons to move it out of our way before my mother finally spoke, "Are you ready, Ana?"

I unsheathed my golden sword and threw the scabbard aside while giving her a grin, "Yeah, I'm ready."

"Cara," my mother spoke again, "are you ready?"

Cara took a deep breath with her eyes focused on me before giving my mother a half hearted nod.

My mother took a few steps back before giving us both one last look.

"Alright then," she finally said. "Begin!"

Cara didn't hesitate. She ran at me swinging her ax but I evaded each swing with minimal effort.

"You're too slow," I told her while quickly jabbing her in the stomach with my free hand. She staggered back from the blow in a way that made me think she was going to fall to her knees, but instead she swiped her ax towards my neck. It would've been a decapitating blow if I wasn't fast enough to duck out of its path. Before she could swing again, I pointed my blade right at her neck forcing her to stop as if she had already lost. I could've killed her right then and there but that obviously wasn't the point of this fight.

"Don't hesitate," I smirked.

"Speak for yourself," she scowled before swinging down her ax in an attempt to split open my skull. I rolled far out of the way to make sure that wouldn't happen, instantly resetting the fight while taking a knee.

"You've gotten faster," she glared me down realizing just how how much the gap between us had widened.

"This is fast for you?" I chuckled while getting myself back up to my feet. "I thought we were just warming up."

She lifted her ax from the cracked stone and got back into position to defend herself.

I raised my sword while telling her, "I guess we have a long way to go before you can reach me."

And without even taking another breath, I bolted straight for her, clashing my sword against her ax. But I didn't stop with the one clash. I kept swinging, causing sparks to fly from her parries. But she was just barely blocking every hit. She was too slow and I needed to push her further.

With a deep breath I felt my muscles tighten. My heart was beating faster and my blood was boiling. To the average person this would've sounded like torture but for some reason I couldn't explain, it made me feel alive. My Warrior's Spirit was activated and I wasn't going to go easy on her.

My body moved faster than even I could comprehend at moments so I could only imagine how Cara was feeling trying to block my strikes. Eventually I got a good hit on her arm, forcing her to drop her weapon. And once again she stopped as if the battle was done.

"Pick it up!" I growled.

"Ana, I—" she started to say but I didn't want to hear it.

Once again I pointed my blade at her neck and repeated, "Pick. It. Up."

She hesitated as she stepped towards it. Her eyes never left me as she knelt down to grasp it. Once she picked it up, she *still* hesitated to hit me with the damn thing.

She finally swiped at me with the ax but I dodged the attack, immediately countering with a jab to her face forcing blood to gush from her nose.

"I said don't hesitate!" I roared while making another attack, this time with my sword. The blade sliced right through her chest. Not too deep but deep enough to draw enough blood to give any warrior a rush.

She stumbled back but didn't want to hesitate. With another desperate attempt she tried to swing her ax with enough power and speed to catch me off guard but I was still able to block the attack, grab her arm, and toss her across the room.

She seemed disoriented as she looked for her weapon until she glanced back at me, finding out that I stole it from her during the toss.

As I strolled towards her with my sword in one hand and her ax in the other she started to crawl away, scooting backwards while pleading, "Ana, wait!"

"To wait is to hesitate," I explained. "You think I'm just going to ignore my own advice?"

"Ana, that's enough!" my mother shouted.

But she was wrong. That wasn't enough. Cara was so close to her limit. She just needed that little *push*.

I smashed the ax down, just narrowly hitting her as she dashed out of its path struggling to keep herself on her feet as she ran.

But I was hot on her trail. I wasn't going to let her run from this. I was going to push her to the brink.

Her back was against the wall. She was defenseless. *Weak.* Just like I was back when I was in the same situation.

I wondered if that's what Barin saw before he stabbed me. No wonder he almost let me go. He felt sorry for me. But luckily I made him change his mind. I made him kill the old me so that I could be reborn as a beast. And I was about to do the same for Cara.

I dashed towards her with my sword ready. Nothing was going to stop me from delivering the finishing blow. Once I swiped my sword through the air, I froze.

It took me a moment to realize what I had done but once it sunk in, it immediately snapped me out of my Warrior's Spirit. I didn't hit Cara. I hit my mother.

Blood was pouring down her face. And her hand... It was completely gone. I looked down to the ground to find it laying in a pool of her blood.

"Mom," I spoke while dropping my blade. "Mom!" I screamed as I inched myself closer to her.

"Stay back!" she shouted in pain and maybe even anger. Or was it fear?

"Why," my voice started to break, "Why would you get in my way? She was fine! She didn't need your help!"

I looked down at Cara, waiting for her to agree with me but she was silent. Blood and tears oozed from her face as she took deep but sharp breaths against the wall. I didn't see the potential warrior I was trying to mold. Just the scared little girl I was trying to kill.

I looked around at the rest of the room. Everyone had a look of terror on their face as if they were staring at a monster.

I looked down at myself and could see Cara's blood on my knuckles and clothes. I could feel my mother's blood on my face.

I turned back to see a couple of women attend to my mothers wounds.

"Wait, let me help!"

"It's ok Ana," one of the women tried to stop me. "We've got experience with wounds like this."

"Well I do too!" I shouted while making my way towards them.

"Ana!" mother roared, forcing me to freeze in place. Then in a much softer and wrenching tone she continued, "Just stand back."

And with that the two women walked past me with my mother and left the room. All I could do was stand there and watch as they tried to fix my mess.

I looked back at the crowd. All eyes were on me. Fearful glares. Stunned anger. Even Cara's eyes had an uneasy disgust to them.

She looked like she was going to say something to me but couldn't find the words. Whatever it was she was going to say, I wasn't ready to hear it.

I turned away from her and ran. I didn't know where I was running to but it had to be anywhere but here.

CHAPTER SIX

KIRA

Eight days had passed since the battle, which was now dubbed, *'The Invasion of Ebony'*. Half of the city was left in ruins and with my father now dead it was up to me to rebuild. But first, we conducted search and rescue to save all that we could.

Many people lost their lives and the ones that didn't were either injured or lost everything in their possession. There were too many to count. Hospitals and shelters began to overflow before morning, so to accommodate them I had to quickly open the gates of the castle to give them refuge. It was one of the few places that was left mostly unscathed during the invasion. It was the perfect place to house those in need while having room to spare.

When it came to decision making, I wasn't alone. Delta and Ranne were right at my side, helping me decide what the best possible moves were for restoring our city. And if we weren't making decisions then we were doing the best we could to just help our people in any way we could.

I walked through the crowded great hall, personally passing out bread to the hungry and medicine to the sick while lugging around a heavy crate with supplies overflowing from it. It was so high to the point where I could barely see what was in front of me.

My leg hit something that felt short and soft. I tripped over it, hitting the ground hard, causing the crate and all the supplies in it to drop and roll across the floor.

"What the hell?" I shouted before looking back to see that I tripped over a small crying child.

"I'm sorry Princess!" the child cried.

Two knights quickly came to my aid, one of them helping me up, and the other roughly grabbing the child by its arm.

"Stop running around you damn brat. How dare you harm the Princess!" The knight shouted.

"No, wait, I didn't mean to! I was just looking for my mom."

The knight looked back at me and said, "I will take care of the kid, Princess."

"No," I told them. "I will deal with the boy. I need you both to pick up these supplies and distribute them evenly among everyone here."

They both bowed and said, "Yes, Princess."

I walked to the young boy and said, "Come, let's take a walk."

As we walked away from the knights he said, "I'm really sorry Princess. I didn't mean to run into you."

"It's fine," I laughed. "Tell me, what were you in such a rush for?"

"I just wanted to find my mother. I don't know where she is."

"Well this is truly a matter that deserves my immediate attention. Don't worry, we'll find your mom," I smiled.

We walked out of the great halls and through the *smaller* halls until we reached the library which in itself ... seemed like just another long hall. But it was wider and filled with tables to sit at. The shelves of books looked like they went on forever and they were trapped behind gates. These books held secrets that no normal person could gain access to. My father only ever let himself and I read from them. He told me that this library was for our bloodline only. Although he did let Delta read some of the books simply because he admired her search for knowledge, he still limited her access to it.

After taking the child deep into the library, we found Delta sitting at one of the tables that were covered with open books. She was hard at work taking inventory and recording all the events that transpired in the last week. I was thankful to have her. Despite only being a child, she was able to keep things organized far better than I ever could.

"Delta," I called. "I need to find this kid's mom."

"What's his name?" she asked.

I looked down at the boy and he answered, "Kian Shadue."

"And your mother's name?"

"Melany Shadue."

"You both have very beautiful names," I told him. "My mother's name was Melany too."

My words made Kian smile for a moment as we waited for Delta to finish flipping through the pages of her book. She finally landed on a page and scanned it before standing up and saying, "Kira, I need to speak with you alone."

She walked a little farther off and I crouched down looking at Kian, "Give us just a moment."

I walked over to Delta and asked, "What's the problem?"

"His mother's dead."

"What? Are you sure?"

"Her body was found and burned yesterday along with the other deceased found."

I looked back at Kian and I didn't know what to say. It was because of me that his mother was dead. I caused so much destruction to this city, but there weren't many people aware of that fact.

Besides Ranne, Crystal, and the rest of her group, it didn't seem like anyone really knew what happened that day. To the public's eyes there was just some random attack by some unknown group. That's all that's known about it. Once I got everything back in order I would answer whatever questions my citizens had, even if it meant that by the end I would be removed from my position.

But now it was time to answer for my crimes much sooner than I expected. I had to answer to this young boy who had lost everything because of me.

As I sat there thinking, I got a glimpse of Ranne walking up to us with a Spirit Caster in hand.

Delta gasped and asked, "Is that—"

"Yup," she cut Delta off before tossing it at her. "The search party finally found your Spirit Caster down at the bottom of the canal."

"Great! I thought I had lost this thing! I can't imagine a world without it." Delta looked over at me and then quickly changed her tone. She could probably tell from the look on my face that I wasn't too thrilled that she had found her Spirit Caster. Mine was completely destroyed in the battle between my father and Crystal. It didn't bother me too much. That Spirit Caster was only good for corrupting its users. I probably would have discarded it either way. But I'd be lying if I said I didn't miss the power. "Sorry Kira," Delta continued.

"No apologies needed," I told her plainly before looking over to Ranne and asking, "How is the search and rescue going?"

"Not good," she answered. "Things aren't progressing fast enough. We need all of our men on this job and we don't have them right now."

"And where exactly are all of our men?"

"Most of our forces are still on Phoenix Island."

"Well, call them back. Conquering Phoenix Island was my father's goal. I need them all here to help every citizen in peril."

"Yes, Princess," she bowed.

"Princess Kira!" We all heard someone shout. We looked over to see a servant run over to us and then plop down on his knees. "Princess, I have urgent news!"

"Well then spit it out. I'm a busy woman."

"Two of the Shēna from the invasion have returned. They demand to speak with you."

"Where are they now?"

"In the great hall. We have them surrounded and they haven't made any hostile moves yet."

"Kira," Ranne said, "this could be dangerous. Should we just imprison them now and interrogate them later?"

"No, I'll meet with them face to face for right now."

"Then we're coming with you."

"So be it."

We all walked out of the library and back to the great hall. I held Kian's hand the entire way, forcing Ranne to ask, "Hey Kira, who's the kid?"

"His name's Kian."

There was a long pause before Ranne asked, "Why is he with us?"

"Because I'm still trying to figure out what to do with him."

"Ok but where did he—"

"Listen, I'll explain it later. The great hall is just up ahead so just be ready for anything."

We turned the corner walking into the great hall and saw all of my knights huddled up into one large group.

"Where are the trespassers?" I shouted.

All of the knights looked back at me and started to make way and in the middle of them all were two Shēna from the invasion. Flint Zapalac and Rai Light.

"Kira!" Flint shouted. "We demand an audience with you!"

It looked like they both meant business, so who was I to deny them that right? I looked at my men and said, "Everyone stand down." I then turned around, "Flint and Rai, come with me."

***

For the first time in my life, I sat on the throne. It was an odd feeling. This was my father's seat. He looked down at me and everyone else from this golden chair. I didn't like this feeling. Maybe if I was still corrupted then I would have reveled in it but now all it did was make me feel even farther from everyone then I already was. I wanted to get this over with as soon as possible.

"Well, you finally have me here," I said. "What do you want?"

"We came here with a couple requests," said Flint.

"Shoot."

"I want you to take your forces off of Phoenix Island. If you don't then we *will* retaliate."

"Already done. I just gave the word to have them all come back right before you trespassed onto my grounds."

He looked shocked by my answer. He was probably expecting a fight but as I said before, I had no desire to conquer his land.

"Well then, I also want you to release the men that I came here with."

"Oh you mean the ones that helped you break in to save your friends? Alright then, I'll pardon them."

Rai finally chimed into the conversation by saying, "I also want you to release my grandmother!"

"That's fair. She hasn't committed any actual crimes so I guess we can do that right now." I then stood up and walked down the steps from my throne before saying, "Come with me."

"Where are we going?" Rai asked.

"Isn't it obvious? We're going to release *everyone*."

***

I led everyone including a small group of knights to the dungeon. Ranne and Delta were still at my side while Flint and Rai were close behind. As soon as we walked through the dark hall every prisoner was on high alert.

It didn't take long for there immediate chatter to turn into shouting.

"Murderer."

"Tyrant!"

"Bitch!"

"You're a monster!"

"Kill yourself!"

These are all statements that I've heard thrown at me at one point or another. But hearing them all at once ... was overwhelming to say the least. So far no one had spoken a single lie. The request to kill myself was justified and a request that I had thought about fulfilling long ago. Maybe it was time to revisit the thought.

I felt the warm touch of Ranne's fingers grazing my back. I did not realize until then but I was shaking. And her touch calmed me. It reminded me that I wasn't alone. That someone, even if it was just one person, cared about me. Not because I was royalty. But because I was me. Because of the person I was *becoming*.

As they all continued their shouting, I took a deep breath and announced, "You're all free to go!"

My words cut straight through the crowd's shouts. They glared at me in pure confusion. Although I had given them good news, I'm sure they still couldn't trust what I was actually saying. But the reality of the situation was that they were free to live their lives.

"Let them out," I told Ranne. She nodded as she passed on the message. All my men spread out to every cell unlocking them all at the same time.

They all came wandering out with caution like scared animals, not sure if they were being led to the slaughter. But one man wasn't so timid. Arnold, the Prince of Phoenix Island strolled right up to face me. The last time we saw each other, we were both under the impression that we would marry each other. Not out of love from my part but out of an obligation for lands to merge and for my father to stretch his rule over that island.

"So, you're just going to let us go?" Arnold asked with a glare. "No catch?"

"You've been locked up for the past week so I guess there's a chance that you might not know the current situation. My father is dead. The King that wanted to take over your land and the scum that you came here to kill is gone. I have no intention to continue in his will so consider your goal accomplished."

As soon as I was about to turn away his escort lunged her hand at me, causing me to flinch my eyes shut. When I opened them I saw that her hand was just an inch away from being wrapped around my throat. The only reason she hadn't wrung my neck was simply because Ranne stopped her by grabbing her wrist. I could I always rely on her reflexes in a pinch.

Ranne's eyes turn red but so did Arnold's escort. I wasn't aware that she *too* was a Zubarian. They both challenged each other using only their glares, but somehow she looked even more intimidating than Ranne. Even without that gigantic lion mane of curls on her head she was still taller than Ranne. Bulkier too.

"Alexia, stand down," the Prince ordered, but she didn't pay him any mind. She simply just turned her attention back on to me.

"You say that you don't intend on continuing his will," Alexia spoke, "but that doesn't change the fact that you still slaughtered our forces and terrorized our innocents in his name. We didn't just come here to kill him. We came here to kill *you.*

Even though I felt safe with Ranne by my side, my throat was still too dry to actually say anything back. And what was I supposed to say? *I'm sorry? I'm not that person anymore?* It doesn't erase anything I've done. I had half a mind to take one step closer, so that she'd have the opportunity to choke the life out of me, if it meant retribution for everyone who's suffered by my hand.

The silence was disrupted by Flint when he came from behind Alexia and wrapped his arm around her shoulder as if they were long time friends.

"Calm down, Lexi," he told her in a relaxed tone. "I asked the Princess to pardon all of you and she very kindly agreed without hesitation. I don't think we should take that for granted."

Alexia looked to him not with anger but with annoyance. Like a sister who didn't want to listen to her older brother. She then groaned and snatched her wrist away from Ranne while deactivating her Warrior's Spirit. She was no longer a threat ... for now.

But as one problem was solved another took its place.

"What do you mean you don't know where she is?" Rai shouted, garnering all our attention.

I walked over to them and asked, "What's going on?"

"We can't seem to find a particular prisoner," a guard answered.

"That doesn't make any sense!" Rai rebutted before looking at me. "You *have* to know where my grandmother is! *You're* the one that locked her up!"

"That's true," I said while looking into the cage. "We did lock her up. Right in this cell. But if she's not here anymore then it must mean she escaped somehow."

"There's no way she could have broken out on her own! You did something to her, didn't you? You didn't keep up your father's end of the deal!"

Suddenly electricity started to surround their body. They were past losing their temper. All that could be felt from Rai was full hostility. Delta pulled out her Spirit Caster and Ranne grabbed onto her sword.

Flint got in-between all of us and said, "Everyone calm down. We don't need to start a fight over a simple misunderstanding."

"Flint's right," I agreed as I rushed beside him. "There are too many civilians in the castle right now for us to start another battle. They've all been through enough already. Do you really want to subject them to more chaos?"

Rai calmed down and the electricity around their body dispersed.

"I'm leaving," they said before storming off.

Flint followed behind them and asked, "Where are you going?"

"I'm going to find my grandmother."

"But you don't even know where she is."

"That's why I'm leaving!" they snapped. "I have no possible idea where she is. She could be back at home safe and sound. Or she could have been kidnapped or stuck in a ditch dying somewhere. Obviously, no one here can help me so there's no reason for me to stick around."

Before Flint could say another word Rai let out the spell, ***"Vima Flas,"*** causing electricity to shoot out of their body and after that, they sped off out of sight in the blink of an eye. Rai really was set on doing this alone. I just hoped that they wouldn't let their rage overtake their emotions. The last thing we needed was Rai getting themselves killed.

CHAPTER SEVEN
CRYSTAL

I sped through the rain as fast as I could on the back of my horse despite how hard it was to see. The moon wasn't out that night, but it shouldn't have been too hard to stay on track since I was staying on a straight path. As I stayed on the trail, I suddenly saw a small glint of light in the distance, and I couldn't tell what it was coming from. The light became brighter and was getting closer at an outrageously quick speed until it finally shot past me like lightning. A thundering boom pierced my ears and forced my horse to stop in its tracks and kick itself up in fear. I fell right off its saddle and into the mud. I started to pick myself up but before I could stand, I heard a voice ask, "Are you ok?"

I looked up and saw one of the last people I expected to see on this journey. "Rai?" I called. Electricity surrounded their body.

They looked down at me with widened eyes and called back, "Crystal? Is that you?" They stretched their arm out to help me up and I took it. The electricity dispersed as soon as I grabbed it.

"What are you doing out here?" I asked.

"I'm going back home to find my grandmother," they answered.

"Tora? Isn't she back in Ebony?"

"No, she's not. Not anymore anyways. And not a single person knows where she's gone off too."

"Wait, *she's* missing too?"

"What do you mean *too*? Who else is missing?"

"Rai, I think we need to talk."

***

Rai and I went back to the same inn that we had hid in after the attack on Ebony. Luckily it wasn't too far from where we met up so it wasn't a long journey. It was also only a day away from Ebony on foot which meant that I wasn't too far from my destination.

We sat at a table in the dark and crowded tavern while wearing cloaks so that we wouldn't stand out. It was a little too lively for my liking. It reeked of beer and sweat and was too loud for us to sit far from each other. But Rai didn't seem to mind. They got themselves a large mug of ale before asking, "Did you want any?"

"Sorry, no." I answered. "I don't drink. Also, aren't you a little young to be drinking yourself? What are you, like fifteen?"

"No. Just turned sixteen the day after we parted ways. And I don't normally drink either, but I'm on edge right now," Rai told me before downing almost half of it and slamming it down to the table. "I need that buzz to help me relieve some of the stress." They wiped their mouth and shook their head before asking, "Who else is missing?"

"My sister Wren, and Alizeh's father."

"Are you serious? *Both* of them along with my grandmother are missing? This can't be a coincidence. Someone had to have taken them!"

"Well, it seems that's actually the case. When Alizeh and I got back, we got into a fight with Arachne Isley, a member of the Five Armaments. And someone else who was working with her. Someone far stronger.

"And that's why you're heading back to Ebony?"

I nodded and said, "I need to question Kira. She might have something to do with all this. You should come with me."

"I already questioned her about my grandmother, and she said she didn't know anything. But your relationship with her is a little more *personal* than mine. You might have better luck getting information out of her," they said before finishing their drink and standing up out of their seat.

"Well if you're not coming with me then what exactly are you going to do?" I asked.

"I'm glad we crossed paths. Because of you I now have a lead. I'm going to find Arachne and get my grandmother back," they answered before slowly starting to walk off. "It sounds like the storm's letting up so I'm going out now. I don't want to waste any time, and I suggest you do the same. If I can't find anything then

I'll come right back to Ebony to see how things are going on your side."

I simply nodded my head as I watched them exit the inn. Once again, I had to watch a friend walk out on me to fulfill their own goals. Each time it made the journey feel more and more lonely since the possibility of seeing them again was so uncertain. But I couldn't let that stop me. We're all trying our best to find the ones we love, so moping around would only slow us all down. I had to take Rai's advice.

I needed to get up, go to Ebony, and find my sister at all costs. Even if it cost me my life. I'll find everyone and get everything back to normal.

CHAPTER EIGHT
ALIZEH

I jumped up out of bed surprised that I was still alive. The last thing I remembered was Barin standing over me with complete blood lust in his eyes. He looked like he was ready to kill me yet there I was, waking up in some random bed in a rundown shelter. The walls looked like they were made of damaged adobe and the room was small and empty. There was a window without glass on the left side of the room where the light shined through making me realize that it was now day. When I looked out of it I saw that I was still in the desert except it wasn't deserted. I was in a town filled with people and buildings like the one I was standing in.

Suddenly I heard the door open and when I looked over I saw Barin coming into the room. I instinctively reached to my side for my Spirit Caster but it wasn't there. He then reached into his cloak and pulled it out while saying, "Looking for this?"

"Give it back!" I demanded.

"No, not yet. You're a lot stronger than I realized and I can still see that rage in your eyes. If I give this back to you now, then you'll probably destroy this entire town without even trying."

I stayed silent because I knew it was true. If I got my Spirit Caster back then I'd probably kill everyone in this town in my attempt to destroy Barin.

He casually walked over to the bed and sat down before asking, "Why are you here?"

"What do you mean? You're the one who brought me here! I don't even know where 'here' is."

"No, I mean what are you doing back in Kítrinos? There has to be a reason. I don't think you came back just to take a little swim in a lake."

I looked at him hard for a good moment before answering in an attempt to calm myself down. "Like I was trying to tell you before, my mother's dying. That jar of water fýkia was the only thing that could've saved her but now because of you it's destroyed!" Despite all my efforts to keep myself composed, tears started to stream down my face.

"That sounds like a rough situation."

"Is that all you have to say?" I shouted. "This is just a 'rough situation'? Not even a *sorry*?"

"I'm not a very empathetic person."

Every time he spoke it only made me more and more enraged. I couldn't hold myself back anymore. I didn't care if I didn't have a Spirit Caster. I wanted to kill him. I ran over to him, grabbed him by his cloak and swung my fist at him as hard as I could, but I was too slow. He easily caught my balled up fist and still had an emotionless look on his face.

"You're a bastard, you know that?" I cried. "You've ruined everything for me, just to satisfy your fragile ego!"

He stared me in the eyes with a different look than before. It wasn't as emotionless. This time it seemed like he was trying to understand *my* emotions. Like he was piecing together a puzzle that should've already been solved.

He finally broke the silence by asking, "How long does your mother have?"

A strange question coming from him. I didn't think he'd care but I still decided to answer anyway. "I don't know. It could be any day now."

"So there isn't much time left." He finally stood up and started untying a pouch that was connected to his hip.

"What are you doing?" I asked.

He then tossed the pouch over to me and said, "Follow me."

I caught it and hesitantly started to open it. I couldn't believe what I found inside. It was gold. And tons of it.

"Are you giving this to me?" I asked him while still focused on the gold. Once I looked back up I saw him exiting the room. I quickly followed behind until we were outside. He pointed over to a large crowd and said, "That's where the market is. I know a vendor there who sells water fýkia. It's expensive but the gold should be more than enough to cover it. Should be able to cover some new clothes and supplies too."

"Wait, you're just giving me your gold to buy this stuff? Why?"

"Because it's not my gold. It's yours. My men stole it from Crystal back when we captured her. I don't have much need for it, so I'm returning it."

"So you're just giving it back with no catch?"

"Oh, there's a catch. I still want that fight. After you save your mother I want you back here so we can settle things."

I pondered the thought for a moment before agreeing to his terms. Since he was helping me I thought it would be wrong to deny him a rematch so I nodded my head, and once I did, he tossed my Spirit Caster back at me.

"When you're done you can find me back in this town. I'll be staying here for a while."

"This all feels a little sudden. I still don't understand why you're just letting me go when there's no guarantee that I'll come back."

Barin's eyes became heavy as he looked at me. He let out a slight chuckle before saying, "I know what it's like to lose a mother. It changes you. And I'd hate to see someone so close to Crystal go through that change. It's not something you can come back from.

For the first time I saw Barin as something more than a monster or some mindless warrior. At that moment Barin seemed human. Like at some point in his life, he might've been somewhat like me. But a simple event turned him into the insane lunatic standing before me. And he was saving me from that same fate. "Thank you for this, Barin. I'll come back as soon as possible for that rematch."

I then turned around and ran off into the crowd. I looked all throughout the market looking for the water fýkia until I finally found a vendor who was selling tons of them in jars. I immediately bought one from him and then worried about my clothes. Because of my meeting with Barin I no longer had any. The only parts I had covered were my chest and my waist. Perfect for swimming alone, but now it just made me feel naked in this sea of people.

I ran to another vendor who had tons of clothes and jewelry hanging from his tarp. I put the sack of gold on his counter and said, "Give me your finest outfit," and after a few minutes he had it all together and I quickly put it on.

I was wearing a black harem skirt which felt wonderful to move in, and it was held up with a golden waist chain. I also had on a sleeveless black crop top with a green poncho right on top of it. The poncho had eagle feathers running along the trim that tickled my skin and made me laugh. And to top it all off I had a golden necklace adorned with green emeralds.

And with that I was finally ready to go. I grabbed my bag of gold and pulled out my wand with the intent to fly off until I heard the vendor say, "Woah, is that a Spirit Caster? I can't believe I'd be selling to two Shēna in the same week. I could've sworn you people went extinct."

I lowered my Spirit Caster and asked, "What was that?"

"Oh, I didn't mean any disrespect. It's just that I've only ever heard stories about you people. I went my whole life without meeting one until recently."

"Who else have you seen? Was it a woman with red hair?"

He shook his head and said "Nah, it was a young man with short black hair and some scary crimson eyes."

Morpheus. It had to be him. There was something menacing in his eyes that made people fear him. He wasn't the person I was looking for but I had a feeling that he was an important piece to the puzzle.

"Do you know where he was going?" I asked.

"Well last I saw him, he was going to the saloon down the road. But that was a few days ago so I doubt he'd still be there."

I looked down the road and took a big sigh. I had to make this detour before leaving. "Thanks for the info," I said before making my way over to the saloon. He probably wasn't there but there had to have been people who had seen him. People who know what he's doing and where he's going. This could be the key to figuring out where my father was so I had to go and see for myself.

I walked through the saloon doors and the place was packed. I wasn't exactly sure who to ask for information, so to narrow it down, I walked over to the bar thinking that the bartender would know something. If Morpheus truly did come through here for a drink then this guy would have definitely talked to him.

I sat at the bar and looked straight at the busy bartender waiting for him to notice me. Once he did, he raised an eyebrow and asked, "You lost kid?"

"No, but I do have a question for you," I answered.

"Well what is it?"

"Have you seen any Shēna come through here?"

"Shēna? You mean those old war criminals? Why's a little girl like you want to know?"

"I have my reasons. The specific one I'm looking for is named Morpheus. He has black hair and red eyes."

"Sorry girly, can't say I have. You should run along now. This is no place for kids."

I took a sigh while getting out of my seat and forgave him for patronizing me. As soon as I turned around to walk out of the saloon I was stopped by a man I've never seen before.

He was tall, dark, and muscular with long black locks like Ana's. His eyes were green, a shade darker than mine and he had metal piercings all over his face. Specifically in his ears, nose, eyebrows and lips. I looked down and saw that he had a sword at his side. But the thing that I noticed before any of that was the massive reserves of Rēa that was flowing from his body.

"Did you just say you were looking for Morpheus?" he asked.

I was surprised to say the least. I had just found another Shēna but not the one I was looking for. And he knew who Morpheus was. I was too shocked to answer him immediately.

"What do you want with him?" he asked.

I wasn't sure if it was wise to answer. For all I knew, he could've been working *with* Morpheus.

Another person came from behind him and said, "Answer the question," in a serious tone. It was a woman. She had on a cloak so it was hard to see her features until she got closer. Her hair was red and her skin was pale. I could feel an overwhelming amount of

Rēa from her too. It was then that everything clicked. The person that was in front of me was none other than Arachne.

She was the one I *really* needed to find. Now that she was in my sights I felt all sense of reason leave my mind and once more all I could see was red. I was going to ask what she did with my father but not before completely pulverizing her.

I took off my backpack and placed it on the floor to ensure that nothing would happen to the plant. They must've sensed my blood lust because they both looked tense. The woman reached to her side most likely in an attempt to pull out her Spirit Caster, but I was much faster on that front.

"Paírno Ptísi," I shouted. Wind burst from behind me and I went flying into her, grabbing her tightly as we darted across the bar and crashed through a window. We flew outside and we both landed and rolled into the sand. Some people around us started to scream and back away before trying to check on us.

A man grabbed onto my arm and asked, "Are you ok?"

I snatched my arm away and shouted, "Get out of here! All of you!" My Spirit Caster started to glow and that got a lot of people's attention.

"She's got a Spirit Caster!" Someone yelled.

"It's a Shēna!" someone else shouted.

"They're both dangerous!" I heard.

And like that everyone scattered like rats. A desired outcome because they were all right. I was dangerous and I didn't want anyone in my way during this fight. If I hurt any of them then it would have weighed heavily on my conscience.

Once I finally got back up, I saw that she was still just lying there. It looked like she was still dazed. I walked up to her and balled my fist.

"Enischyméni Michanikí Diátrisi."

Wind balled around my fist. One hit with this to her temple in her current state meant that she wasn't getting back up for a while, if at all.

Once I was standing right over her I raised my fist and was just about to slam it down into her skull until I felt something wrap around it. It was a metal chain. I looked behind me to see the other Shēna holding the other end of the chain. Then he yanked it with so much force that I was sent hurtling towards him. I knew he was setting up another attack so I surrounded myself in Rēa, but before I could think to do anything else, he punched me dead in the cheek, forcing me to partially sink into the sand. I never felt a more greater pain before that punch. Pretty sure he cracked a tooth.

"Stay down," the man demanded. "I don't want to kill you so just give up and tell us what we want to know."

I hated that. His condescending tone. Everyone's constantly patronizing me because I'm a child. And that was starting to infuriate me!

"Anemostróvilos!"

A large tornado spewed from my body and flung him into the air. I stood up and looked down at my Spirit Caster. I was shocked to see that once again it was evolving. I looked around and started to see bricks from houses being torn apart, vendor shops being toppled down. This spell was too powerful to use in a space like this. I had to stop it and suppress my power. I concentrated and stopped the evolution, causing the new parts of the Spirit Caster to turn to dust and blow away with the wind. Then the tornado finally stopped and the sky's were clear from my spell but were covered with another one.

I looked up and saw something raining down. They were gleaming in the sunlight and for a second I couldn't make them out but once I did, my heart skipped a beat. They were swords. Hundreds of them. Raining down from the sky as if God's soldiers were all ready to attack Earth.

"Grígoros Ánemos!" I shouted. I jumped back darting from one spot to another in order to avoid these blades until finally one sliced my arm. And then another one hit my leg. If I was going to survive then staying grounded wasn't my best option. I had to go straight to the source. I looked up into the sky and saw the man standing on top of some strange metallic platform. I didn't understand what kind of Spirit Caster he had to be pulling off such a powerful and amazing move, but I guess it didn't matter. Just like my first ever real battle against Adam, my only option was to close the gap and give him one finishing blow.

"Paírno Ptísi." The spell lifted me up and I started flying towards him while narrowly dodging most of the falling blades. I ended up with a few scratches but nothing too serious until one blade seemingly came out of nowhere and grazed my left eye. It almost made me spin out of control but I stopped myself. I couldn't see out of one eye, but that wasn't going to stop me when I was so close to him.

I continued my pursuit for him until I finally made it past every sword. There was nothing else in the way between me and him. I raised my hand and shouted, ***"Gale Lance!"*** This was going to be the finishing blow.

Once I got closer he stretched his hand up into the air and I could see his mouth moving. He was getting ready for an incantation. Something big was coming. I didn't know how big it was until he actually spoke the spell.

"Pylónas Sidírou."

Then the sky went black. For a moment my blurred vision made me think that he had somehow made it night. But then I realized that he had put something in the sky that was so large, it blocked out the sun. It was a giant floating pillar.

Fear struck through my body and paralyzed me. My most recent spell fizzled out, causing the small tornado of piercing wind to disperse from my hand, and I felt defenseless. Then with a flick of his wrist he gestured towards me and the pillar started to fall from the sky.

I didn't know what to do. I didn't know how to stop it. I didn't know if I *could* stop it or even *avoid* it!

I tried to think of a spell but I wasn't fast enough. The giant iron pillar weighed itself down against me and pushed me back down towards the earth. As soon as I hit the sand I could see only black, and the last thought I had was the overwhelming fact that I was weak. I was just a child. And because of that and so many other factors ... I was now the loser of this battle.

CHAPTER NINE
ANA

I sat against the wall, staring into the warm fire. The only source of light in the dark cave. It was the same cave that Crystal and I had hid in after our first meeting with the Princess. The first place I had ever gone to run and hide. It's funny how things come full circle like that.

I was lost in thought as I looked into the fire. So lost that I didn't hear them come in. Without even thinking I pulled out my dagger and pointed it right at the shadowy figures standing past the entrance of the cave.

"You made it pretty far out here on foot," Cara sighed as she threw her heavy bag to the floor.

"How'd you find me?" I questioned.

"Do you really have to ask?" she questioned back as Silver strolled up to me in order to sniff and lick my hair. I didn't push him away but I didn't feel like acknowledging him either.

"You shouldn't have followed me," I told her.

"We were worried about you. Last time you left without saying a word, you were gone for months. And you came back with only one eye."

I glared at her with said eye, causing her to rethink that last statement.

"What?" she asked. "Too soon?"

I ignored her question to ask another, more pressing one of my own.

"How's my mother?"

"Also worried."

"You know what I mean, Cara."

She looked down at the floor and bit the inside of her cheek before looking back up at me and telling me, "She'll live."

A vague answer but satisfying for now. I looked away from her and back into the flames since there was nothing else I had to say to her. Nothing else I *could* say. Not after what I did.

"Look, Ana," she started to make her way over to me, "I'm sorry."

"What do you have to be sorry for?" I asked, not taking my eyes off the flame.

"You put your faith in me to help you get stronger. And I failed to meet those expectations. I couldn't measure up to where you needed me to be. And in the end, because of *my* weakness, your mother suffered for it."

"Cara," I snapped my head towards her direction. "Nothing that happened yesterday was your fault...*I* got greedy. And selfish.

And I pushed you farther than I should've. All for my own sake. *That's* why my mother got hurt. And if she didn't get in the way, then you would've died by my hands. I don't think I could've lived with that. I can barely live with *this*."

"I can't live with it either. Being so weak I mean. Having to be saved by everyone else. I'm tired of it. Ana, I wanna get stronger...I wanna try again."

I stared deep into her determined eyes and asked, "Try what again?

She crouched down until our eyes were at the same level.

"I wanna fight you to the death. One more time."

"Cara," I looked away from her with my body tensing from the memory of our last bout. "I can't."

"What do you mean you can't? That's what you wanted from the beginning right?"

"I don't want to fight anymore."

"Seriously?" she scoffed. "*You* of all people don't want to fight? That's like, your whole thing."

"I'm serious. People got hurt because of me."

"And you're just going to let us get hurt in vain? If we don't get anything out of it then it will all be for nothing."

"Cara," I sighed, but she didn't let me get another word in.

"And regardless," she continued. "If you're really that sorry then you'll help me get stronger. You owe it to me." And without even waiting for an answer she got back up and started to walk away.

"Where are you going?" I asked.

"Me, you and Silver are heading back to the temple."

"You know I can't do that."

Cara took a moment to roll her eyes and then turned back to sit next to me.

"Fine," she groaned, "we'll leave when you're ready."

"I won't be going back," I warned.

"Then I guess that means we'll be staying a while," she added while leaning back on the wall.

I thought she would've hated me for what I did but there she was, waiting by my side the same way Silver would at one of my lowest points. I wonder if I could say the same about my mother. I'd never had to question such a thing before but now things were different. *I* was different. I turned into a monster who needed to keep itself on a leash.

***

I woke to the smell of burnt wood and what sounded like an axe thumping against a tree. It was morning just outside the empty, dim cave. I slowly got up and stretched my muscles that were sore from laying on the solid foundation and made my way out to the snowy woods.

I followed the sound, pushing through the brush until I found Cara swinging her ax against a tree that was hanging on by a thread. Silver, who was once patrolling the area, quickly strutted his way over to give me his wet kisses.

"Good morning to you too," I chuckled while rubbing his neck.

Soon the tree came crashing down along with the beads of sweat falling from Cara's forehead. I thought it was odd for her to be so worn out after just chopping down one tree until I looked around to see an entire path of broken trees and strips of wood.

"You've been busy," I assumed.

"I didn't know how long you were going to sit here and pout, so I just wanted to get our firewood situation out of the way."

'Sit here and pout'? I repeated the words in my mind. Is that actually what it looked like I was doing? That must've been weird to see from the outside. For *me* of all people to be so shaken. So fragile. So scared.

It's not the way I wanted to be perceived. To Cara, all of this was a waste of time. The thought of just dropping this and listening to her crossed my mind but not for long.

Silver's growling put my body in fight or flight. Cara and I turned to see something moving in the distance. It was big, and it was coming at us fast. Once it got close I realized exactly what I was looking at. The only thing that would rival a wolf like Silver. A white bear.

I glanced back at Cara to see her frozen at the sight of it. We had a run in with a much smaller one a few years back and she looked just as scared then as she did now. Once again I needed to step up.

"Cara, stand back!" I ordered as I slowly made my way towards the bear. My muscles tensed up in an attempt to activate my Warrior's Spirit, but nothing happened. I felt no boost in power. My blood wasn't rushing from excitement, but instead from fear.

I tried it again. Still nothing. Over and over again, I tried in a panic to get my power going until the bear was just meters away. And for the first time in a long time, I felt truly helpless.

Before I knew it, the bear was just a second away from trampling me before Cara lunged towards me, pushing us both out of its path. The bear came to a grinding halt to glare at us as we both got back up to our feet. It was going to go in for another charge until Silver decided to go on a charge of his own, pushing the beast away from us.

I looked down at my hands and balled them into fists, gaining Cara's attention.

"Ana?" she asked in a panic. "What's wrong?"

"My Warriors Spirit," I choked. "I can't ... I can't feel it."

I looked back up at Silver. He was being pounced on by the beast as it's claws tore through his flesh. I wanted to kill it. I wanted to stop it. But for the first time since the day my father died, I felt true fear born from the powerlessness of my blood.

Cara had no such weakness. She ran towards the two animals while swiping her ax from off the ground and a rock along with it. She tossed the rock right at the bear's face while screaming, getting its attention just long enough for Silver to claw at its face forcing the bear to claw back.

They were both in sync trying to take the heat off of the other. And they both fought with their natural strength. No need for some boosted power up from their spirit. I snapped out of my fear and ran after them, arming myself with the biggest stone I could find.

Cara lunged at the beast, slicing down on its neck with her ax, but the cut wasn't deep enough. It tried to snap at her with its fangs, almost getting her arm before I jumped on its back, completely diverting its attention.

I raised the rock up with all the strength I could muster and slammed it right down on its skull, breaking the stone in two. It barely made more than a bloody scratch. It was just a scratch but you know what the say about a beast that can bleed. So I raised the broken slab up to go for another attack, but the bear was quick to push me off into the snow just by standing on its hind legs.

It was a gigantic beast. At least two times taller than Cara and I. With its weight alone all it needed to do was slam down its paw on my head for me to never see the light of day again. But silver stopped that before it could become a reality.

My wolf pounced on the bear causing them both to roll down the hill as if both the white haired creatures were a part of the snow that formed into an avalanche.

This time I didn't hesitate to help my friend. I jumped up and ran after the two as Cara followed close by my side.

They both stopped rolling just short of the edge of a cliff. Silver started to get up but the white bear was faster. It lunged itself at Silver, but I did the same, vaulting over Silver's saddle while simultaneously drawing my sword from it. And within the same motion, I slashed deep into the bear's face, taking out its left eye.

It definitely felt that one as it stumbled back with a roar of pain. Cara took that opportunity to go for its other eye, slamming her ax right into the side of its face.

Even though the poor beast couldn't see, it still charged at her. She narrowly rolled out of its path letting it run right off the cliff, and tumble down to certain doom.

Cara fell down into the snow while shouting, "*Great Sister Gods*, I can't believe we're still alive!"

My whole body shook from fear and adrenaline as I dropped to my knees trying to compose myself.

"We're only alive thanks to you," I told her.

"*Me?*" she repeated.

"Yes. *You,*" I confirmed. "You were the first one to make a move. And the last. I was powerless without my Warriors Spirit."

Cara sat up while saying, "Don't sound so grim. You've awakened it before. You'll do it again."

"But who knows how long that'll take."

Cara looked at me and said, "I think I know a way to jump start it."

I looked back at her, already having a feeling of what she was going to say.

"Ana," she spoke. "Let's have a battle to the death."

CHAPTER TEN
CRYSTAL

Even though the sun had risen, the sky was still black over Ebony. Smoke and heat rose from the flames that covered parts of the city and blackened the clouds, forcing it to rain. People crowded the streets while heading towards the castle. My guess was that Kira made it a refuge from the disaster. The one that *we* caused.

But maybe I was being too hard on myself. I didn't lay a finger on this city. Throughout my fight, the only person that caused any destruction was Kira herself. But I guess she wasn't in control when that happened. And I was the one who pushed her to become that demon of destruction. Debatably, I was just as guilty as she was, if not more. And I was sure that the people of Ebony would have had the same opinion, so I kept my hood covering up most of my distinctive hair along with some of my face, and stared straight as I rode my horse.

Once I made it to the castle gates, I went right into the courtyard and saw something that made me linger. It was a wall of ice. The same one that I made to protect Flint and Rai in the last battle. It was still standing. Albeit a bit smaller than before, but still standing. It was almost like a memorial. A reminder that the effects from our war were still here, towering over everyone it had hurt.

I hopped off my horse and made my way to the castle doors. They were open as civilians flocked through the entrance. I followed suit and once I made it through those doors I saw even more side effects of the war.

It was crowded in the grand hall. Families huddled together around those who were injured to pray over them. Soldiers and servants were running around like chickens with their heads cut off trying to handle all of the hungry. There was a stench in the air. Not just that of people who haven't been able to clean themselves but a stench of death. Our battle took more casualties than I would have ever expected.

The more I thought of it, the more it made me want to scream. I had to shake it off. I didn't come to the castle to mourn. I came to find my sister.

I quickly walked through the hall in order to try and find Kira while passing by many of the injured, avoiding eye contact with everyone I came across. I shoved my way through crowd after crowd constantly apologizing before I ran into one person in particular.

I bumped right into him and said, "Sorry I didn't mean to—"

"Crystal?" The boy asked, interrupting me.

The familiarity of his voice forced my eyes to look into his. Their golden eyes calmed me. "Flint?" I asked, before embracing him with a hug. "You're ok!"

"Of course I'm ok. It's *me* we're talking about."

I pulled away while still holding him. "What are you doing here?"

"I came here to ask Kira if she could pardon all of the people I came here with," he answered.

"You mean the ones that helped you save us?"

"Yup."

"And how is that working out for you?"

He turned me around and gestured towards a large group of people close to us. "It worked out just fine. She let them all go without a hitch. Well, *almost* without a hitch."

I looked back at him and asked, "What do you mean?"

Flint took a deep sigh before saying, "She couldn't let go of Rai's grandmother."

"I heard. Rai told me on my way here."

"Wait, you talked with Rai?"

"Yeah, I did. And it seems that Rai, Alizeh, and I have the same problem."

"And what problem would that be?"

"We're all missing someone close to us."

"Who else is missing?"

"Alizeh's father, and my sister."

Flint's eyes became more serious as he said, "This doesn't sound like a coincidence."

"It's not. This was planned. All I know at the moment is that two Shēna were involved. One of them being Arachne Isley."

Flint's eyes widened. "I know her. Alizeh and I fought her. I gave her the finishing blow, but I was too weak to check if she was *actually* finished. So that must be why you're here?"

I nodded my head and said, "I need to talk to Kira about this. If she actually has turned over a new leaf then I think having her help me sort this all out will fix things way quicker than trying to piece this together on my own."

"Well I can't argue with that. We should go ask her now."

"Do you know where she is?"

He nudged his head over to the other side of the room. I looked over and saw her with another family. She was handing them a loaf of bread and consoling them. It was strange to see the woman I once knew as an evil, cold blooded killer turn into a kind, loving Princess with an actual heart.

As Flint and I walked across the hall he asked, "By the way, where is Ana and Alizeh?"

"Oh Ana? She should be back in Nótio Págo by now."

"Oh, so she's not with you? That's a shame. I came all this way to save you guys and I didn't even get a chance to see her off."

"If it makes you feel any better, she feels the same. She would've stayed with you while you were hurt if she hadn't left her mother waiting for so long."

"That's pretty funny to think about considering the fact that she's always playing so hard to get when she's around me. She treats me like I'm just another fling."

The thought made me giggle before saying, "Don't overthink it, Flint. She's crazy for you."

That put a big smile on his face that he tried desperately to hide. He switched the conversation.

"And what about Alizeh? I'm guessing since her dad is missing, she must be here looking for him too?"

"Unfortunately, no. Her father wasn't the only one in danger. They may have left her mother behind but sadly we found her poisoned, and she's only got days until it kills her. Alizeh's currently searching for a cure."

"Man, this all keeps getting worse and worse. That means we're on the clock."

Once we finally got within earshot to the Princess I called her name.

"Kira!"

She looked back at me and the warm smile that she gave to the family faded away. She turned back to them and said, "You'll have to excuse me. There's some important business I have to attend to."

She then grabbed one of the children's hand and walked over to me before saying, "Crystal Winters. To what do I owe the pleasure?"

"I need you to tell me where Arachne is," I told her.

"Arachne? Probably dead," she said bluntly. "I assumed that one of you killed her. I haven't seen her since our last battle."

"She's not dead."

"And what makes you think that?"

"Because Arachne took my sister and Alizeh's father."

"What do you mean she took them?"

"Exactly what it sounds like. Our family members were kidnapped by a member of your team. She's probably the one behind Tora's disappearance too. If you want to make things right then you should think real hard about where she could possibly be."

Kira's expression somehow got more serious than before. "I have no idea where she could possibly be. Arachne and Morpheus were nowhere to be found after our battle. We all just assumed they were both dead but considering that Morpheus is the master of illusions," she trailed off before looking back at me and saying, "you should come with me."

She turned around and started walking in the opposite direction. Flint and I took a quick glance at each other before deciding that we didn't really have another choice. Even though she was a killer who I so desperately wanted to put down, we had to trust her.

After spending an overly large amount of time following Kira through the massive halls of the castle, she finally stopped in front of a large set of doors before turning and giving me a key.

"This is Arachne's room. Morpheus's room is just down the hall. This key will open both doors. You can go in and do as much investigating as you'd like. This is the most I'll be able to do for you at the moment. Now if you'll excuse me, there are other things that need my attention."

"Thank you," I told her before she left us.

Flint and I went inside of the room and saw that it was classy, yet *disgusting*. Lots of space filled with fancy furniture while empty bottles of fine wines were scattered all amongst the room like trash.

"Looks like Arachne lived a life full of debauchery," I assumed.

"I don't blame her," said Flint as he picked up a bottle. "It's the kind of life I would have chosen if *I* were a part of the Five Armaments."

"We're not here to fantasize about a better life," I scoffed. "We're here because lives are on the line. Take this key and go check out Morpheus's room. If Kira thinks it's worth checking then one of us should be on top of it while the other checks in here."

"Good idea, but what exactly are we looking for?"

"Anything that could lead us to them. Whether it be some piece of writing or simply if something just seems off."

"Do you think they would just leave a trail like that behind?"

"If my childhood back in Nótio Págo has taught me anything, it's that wild beasts always leave a trail. Finding said trail requires a keen eye that doesn't overlook even the most minute of details."

"You know they're not animals right?"

"Trust me. We're definitely dealing with animals," I assured him while looking at the mess of the room. "Now go."

He turned around and walked out of the room leaving me alone to myself. This was my chance to finally get down to business. I made my search around the room, looking in her drawers and closet only to see clothes. I looked under most of her furniture and only found dust. I looked at her desk and found something of interest. A locked drawer.

I didn't have a key so I had to rely on the next best thing. I took out my Spirit Caster, tapped it against the lock and said, ***"Droserós."***

The lock started to freeze over and once it did I crushed it with my Rēa, forcing it to shatter. Once I opened the drawer I found a stack of letters all from one person. Someone named Amethyst, and she claimed to be her sister. There were too many letters to sort through, but I saw a continuous pattern between the letters. They seemed to be focused on Morpheus. This person, Amethyst, didn't want Arachne mixed up with him. Apparently Morpheus was a mad man who wanted to become a god. I didn't see anything about what he was actually planning to do or where he wanted to do it. But this confirmed it. Whatever is happening is all Morpheus's doing. Whatever their goals are, it's one and the same.

Soon Flint came back into the room and said, "Crystal, I found something."

"What is it?" I asked.

"I think you'll want to see for yourself."

I got up and followed behind. Once we walked into Morpheus's room, I saw a bunch of papers tacked onto one of the walls. I walked up to them and saw maps and words like, 'sacrifice' and 'phoenix feathers' written all over them.

"All this was hidden behind a large wardrobe," Flint explained. "I have no idea what this psychopath is planning, but it seems pretty big."

I glared at the wall studying it for a moment before finally looking back at Flint and saying, "The Princess needs to see this."

After a stressfully long wait, we finally got Kira, Delta, Ranne ... and strangely enough the random child who I've seen stuck to Kira's hip ever since I got to the castle. But I guess it didn't matter all that much in the situation, so I didn't ask about him.

"This is all very interesting but I still don't think I can help you," said Kira.

"All the information here doesn't really show us what his plan actually is," Ranne added. "It has names of places I've never even heard of." She walked over to one specific word and pointed at it. "Like this one right here. **'Skoteinós Kósmos'.** Has anyone here ever even heard of that?"

"I have." Delta said, arousing everyone's attention.

"What is it?" I asked.

"Another world apparently. It comes up a lot in the books I've read in the castle's library but I don't know too much about it."

We all glanced at each other. *Another world?* It sounded almost far-fetched.

"Do the books not have any actual information on it?" Flint asked.

"Not the books I've read. I wanted to learn more about it but it seemed to be classified information hidden by the king. He locked them behind a gate so no one could read them."

"Well luckily for us my father's dead," Kira said. "I am soon to be Queen of this continent. So I decide what is and isn't classified. Delta, take us to these books."

"Yes, my Queen."

CHAPTER ELEVEN
RAI

I ran around the Black Continent throughout the night, looking for answers by interrogating people from town to town about where I could find the Shēna who took my grandmother. Although the only breaks I gave myself were small naps throughout the next day, I still found the energy to keep on searching. I didn't have any time to waste.

Eventually my travels brought me to a town hidden in a forest filled with giant trees that stretched towards the sky. Although the village was dark from all the shade, it was still lively. Animals wandered along with people as if they lived as one. Children played on the dirt path as adults were hard at work gardening and farming. The town I had found was named Kardiá and it was right in the center of Livádia which was fitting. Not only was it the capital of Livádia, but it felt like it's heart.

I walked through the small town until I finally reached an inn; a perfect place for interrogations. I walked through and once I saw that the place was full and lively I shouted, "I'm looking for a Shēna!" That forced everyone to become silent and stare at me. Most of my sources led me here so I knew they had to be in this town.

"Well? Where are they?" I shouted.

One large man got up and asked, "Who wants to know?"

"Does it matter?"

"Yeah, it does."

Another man stood up and they both started to walk towards me. "What do you want with them?" he asked. They were both in my face now. "If you're here to harm them then you'll have to get through us."

I didn't have time for this.

"Víma Flas."

Electricity surrounded my body as I kicked the first man right in his face causing him to crash onto the floor. I grabbed the other man by his neck, raised him up in the air and then slammed him through a nearby table.

"If someone in here doesn't tell me where they are in the next couple of seconds then I'm going to start getting angry."

The electricity around my body got more ferocious, causing people to duck under tables and hide behind the counter.

"Wait!" The innkeeper yelled. "They're over by the lake at the edge of town. There's only one house there, you can't miss it. Just please don't cause us any more trouble."

And like that, I turned around to make my exit, but before I could, the man continued saying, "Also, please don't hurt them."

I turned back around to look at him and asked, "What was that?"

"They're good people," one person said.

"They don't deserve this!" Another man yelled.

"Please show some mercy and just leave."

I wondered if Arachne also had the ability to poison peoples' brains. I didn't understand what they could have done for these people to want to protect them so badly. Either way I still needed to find them and make them pay.

Not too long after, I finally made it to the lake. The innkeeper was telling the truth. I could *feel* them. There was an equal chance that they already felt me coming as well, but it wouldn't hurt to take extra precautions. I powered down and approached the house slowly using any cover I could find. I went around the back and snuck into the bushes with my Spirit Caster drawn and ready to attack whoever was unfortunate to come out of that cottage.

Once I got close enough, I saw a child with scruffy blond hair and green eyes. He looked no older than Alizeh. It made me doubt whether or not I even sensed them here, because I knew for a fact that this wasn't the person I was looking for.

He was carrying a withered, potted plant. My first thought was that maybe he was going to throw it away since it looked like it was at the point of no return. But something else a lot more interesting happened. He took out a Spirit Caster and uttered the word, ***"Therapévo."***

The plant started to slowly stand up straight and get its color back. After just a few seconds, the plant was in perfect health. I slowly stood up to get a better look.

"Amazing," I said.

The boy was startled after he noticed me and then had a look of panic in his face.

"Hey kid," I continued, "don't look so grim. I'm not gonna hurt you. I'm just curious about that power of yours."

Right at that moment, the back door opened and a woman came out saying, "Aeson you should get back inside, it's going to get dark soon."

Once she caught sight of me the same grim look fell upon her face and she ran to her son grabbing him and asking him, "Are you ok?" He nodded his head and she looked back at me. "What do you want? Are you with the other two?"

"Other two?" I asked

"Morpheus and Arachne! Are you with them?" She asked while bringing the boy in close.

She knew Morpheus and Arachne personally? This only proved I was on the right track.

"No, I'm not with them."

"Then why are you here?"

"Because I heard rumors that there were Shēna in this area and I thought it might be them. But now I know that those so-called Shēna are you guys."

"Well if that's the case then you should be on your way."

"Wait, what did they do to you?" I asked. The question made her give me an angry look but I still pressed on. "They took someone from me and I'm trying to get them back. So please if there's anything you can tell me about them or where they are then I'm begging you. *Please* just talk to me."

"They took someone from you too?" The woman's eyes softened as she loosened her grip on the boy. "Would you like to come inside?"

***

A bit of time passed once we were settled into the cabin. I sat in a chair with a cup of tea in hand as she sat in another. Aeson was told to stay in his room as we talked.

"You should drink every last bit of that tea. You've probably had a long journey and that gray tea will replenish your energy."

"I'm not too big on tea," I responded. "My grandmother would force me to drink it all the time. It tasted just like this too."

"Then your grandmother is wise. That kind of tea will boost the Rēa reserves in a Shēna. We used to drink it all the time before going into battle."

I looked down at the cup and decided to take her advice, slowly sipping on it throughout the conversation.

"So I'm guessing you're pretty knowledgeable about this kind of stuff. The human body I mean."

"Yes, I am. I'm actually the town doctor. Or at least I was the town doctor. Truth is I'm getting too old for that job. So I decided to pass on the torch to someone younger."

"And I'm guessing that certain someone is your son?"

"Precisely. But he's not my only son. I have another boy named Thelonious. He's much older, almost a man now. He trained for that position his entire life, but I didn't give it to him. He had too much greed in his heart. His younger brother Aeson was much more pure. So I decided to give the title and the Spirit Caster to him instead."

"It sounds like you made the right choice."

"I'm not too sure about that. Maybe if I would have given him the Spirit Caster he wouldn't have left."

"I'm sorry to hear that, but I think that we should get to the more pressing matter at hand. Morpheus and Arachne."

"Ah yes those two. They were the ones that took him."

"What? They took him too?" I asked, almost spilling my drink.

"Let me explain exactly what happened. A few days ago, Morpheus and Arachne came to my door trying to recruit my sons for some crazy scheme. He offered them power beyond their wildest dreams. He told them that they would become gods as long as they would pledge their allegiance to him. Aeson refused as expected but Thelonious actually considered it. Then they promised to give him his own Spirit Caster that they claimed to be stronger than mine. Once he heard that, he agreed and left with them."

"So Morpheus is just taking Shēna to make some kind of army? But if that's the case then I don't understand why he would take my grandmother. She's too old to fight for him."

"Tell me," she started to ask, "What is your grandmother's name?"

"Tora," I told her.

Her eyes widened before asking, "Leoht?"

"You knew her?"

"Yes actually. We used to be good friends. It's pretty scary to think they got their hands on her."

"Which is why it's important for you to tell me exactly where they're going."

"They're going to Nótio Págo," we heard someone say from the other side of the room. Aeson came from around the corner fully dressed, and with a backpack on. "There's a temple there that they said they were going to. But before you leave I need you to take me with you."

"You're a healer, right?" I asked, interested at the proposal. "That could be useful. Alright then, I'll let you tag along."

The boy's face brightened before his mother shouted, "You will be doing no such thing!"

The boy looked like he wanted to say something back. He wanted to argue so badly but couldn't find the words. He seemed timid but there was something in his eyes that I liked. I looked back at his mother and said, "I'll probably need his help."

"Really?" they both said in unison with the boy being more surprised than his mother.

"Yes. If I go alone I'll be easily overpowered by the three of them. But if your son is there to help as support then my chances of winning are boosted by a large margin."

"But, what if he gets hurt?"

"I won't let that happen."

She looked at me with an analyzing look and asked, "How can you be so sure? Are you even as strong as Tora?"

"If you're talking about when she was in her prime, then I'm probably stronger."

"Strength isn't everything. This is also about experience. And you don't look like you've been in too many fights."

I placed my tea cup on the table and leaned in a little closer to make sure she heard the next words I was about to say.

"I helped kill the King."

There was a long silence in the room as she attempted to process what I had just said.

"The assault on Ebony... that was you?"

"Along with a few others. I needed help beating the King and I'm going to need help again when it comes to beating Morpheus. Since everyone who previously helped me are scattered far and wide, it's too inconvenient for me to gather them in a timely manner. Your son is the best help I can possibly get right now."

She let out a deep sigh as she thought it over. "You better not make me regret this." She looked over at Aeson and told him, "You can go with Rai if that's what you really want, just be careful."

Aeson had a bright smile and looked at me while saying, "I won't disappoint you."

"That's good to hear. Make sure you get some rest. We leave at dawn."

CHAPTER TWELVE
CRYSTAL

Skoteinós Kósmos. An entire dimension shrouded in darkness, said to have been created by the gods to leave this world behind. It seemed impossible for me to believe, but at this point in my life, the word *'impossible'* had no meaning.

I flipped through page after page of the sacred text searching for a way to get there. I started to wonder if there even *was* a way to enter this world. Morpheus could've just been crazy to think that he could actually set foot in it.

"Any luck?" Flint asked while coming to my side with a cup in hand.

I grabbed it and said, "No, not yet."

I took a sip from the cup and realized it was hot cocoa, my favorite.

He looked over at the large windows on the walls. It was night and the only thing lighting the library were candles.

"It's late," he said. "Sure you don't wanna take a break?"

"This isn't like last time. Before, we weren't on a ticking clock, but now we are. People's lives are on the line. *Wren's* life is on the line. There's so many people counting on me to figure this out. I can't stop. Not until I find her."

I turned the page of the book and saw a map of sorts that I didn't truly understand. It looked more like a labyrinth than anywhere that seemed familiar. At one point on the map, there was a black '**X**' that marked a spot with the word 'Doorway' right under it.

"What's this supposed to be?" he asked.

"I don't know."

We brought it to Kira's group to see if they knew anything about it.

Kira and Delta couldn't quite put their fingers on what it was, but Ranne could.

"They're underground tunnels beneath the castle," she explained. "This map looks like it will lead us to whatever we're looking for."

"How do we get there?" I asked.

"There's a manhole right in the center of the courtyard that leads you right to it."

"How do you even know that?" Kira asked.

"Those tunnels are the entryway to the underground arena that your father made me fight in to test my abilities."

Kira looked surprised at the information as if it gave her more clarity into something that was much more personal than I could understand. But that topic didn't have anything to do with my sister, so I tried to keep the conversation on track.

"So you're pretty familiar with the tunnels?"

"Unfortunately no. I just know how to get to them. It's pretty close to the castle, but he never let anyone actually explore past the arena."

"Wait, if the entrance is so close then that means Morpheus is probably already there."

"It's definitely a high possibility," Delta agreed.

"Then we're going now." Kira ordered. "Ranne, lead the way."

***

Ranne led us out of the castle and into the courtyard. Our cloaks shielded us from the rain while our boots were muddied from walking through the grass. Ranne stopped and bent down to the ground, picking up the heavy looking manhole cover and throwing it to the side.

"This is it," she told us.

"I'll go down first," I said before descending the long ladder. It didn't take too long for me to reach the bottom of the flooded tunnel with water that reached up to my knees. Flint came down right behind me and then the rest of the group did the same.

"I can barely see anything down here," I complained.

Flint raised his Spirit Caster up and said, ***"Flóga Dóry."*** Flames burst out of both ends of his staff like a double edged torch, lighting our surroundings. He then looked at us and asked, "Where's the map?"

"I've got it," I told him, while raising it up.

"Well then, lead the way," he gestured to the darker parts of the tunnel. I nodded my head and stepped in front of the group ready to lead them through the dark and foreboding path.

It took some time to reach the halfway point of our journey, traveling through the twists and turns of the flooded cave. It felt never ending, but we were getting close. Even so, I still didn't feel safe. It felt like something was in there with us. It gave me shivers.

Suddenly Delta stopped in place, turned around facing the opposite end of the tunnel, and pulled out her Spirit Caster.

"What is it?" Kira asked.

"There's something in the water," Delta answered. "I can feel it. We're being followed."

I couldn't see anything behind us, but being that she has control over water meant that I wasn't going to doubt her. I pulled out my Spirit Caster just as everyone braced themselves for whatever was coming for us.

Soon we heard splashing. Whatever it was, it was getting closer.

"Get behind me, Kira," Ranne said as she drew her sword.

We were all ready to attack until the thing finally showed its face. It wasn't really a *thing* and more of a person. A child to be exact. It was the same black-haired child from before. The same boy who was with Kira. Even though it meant we were safe it still was unsettling to see him. His crimson eyes reminded me of Kira's and it almost made me squirm.

"Kian, what are you doing here?" Kira asked in a stern voice almost as if she were his parent. "I thought I told you to stay in the castle!"

"Kira," I interrupted, sick of being in the dark on this situation, "who the hell is this kid? He's been attached to you like a son with his mother. What, is he some kind of secret love child you had before meeting Ranne?"

Kira blushed and quickly said, "No, it's nothing like that! He's one of the survivors from our battle and he's been separated from his parents. I wanted him by my side until I could figure out what to do with him and others in a similar situation." She then turned back to him and asked again, "What are you doing down here?"

"Forgive me, Queen Kira. I just didn't want to be alone."

Kira scowled at him but ended up saying, "Fine, you can stay with us."

"Kira," Ranne interjected. "Are you sure that's the best idea?"

"No, not the best, but it would be too much trouble to turn back now," Kira grabbed his hand and pulled him closer to us. "Let's continue on."

"No," Delta said in a serious tone.

"Why not?" Kira questioned.

"Because Kian wasn't the only thing I felt in the wa—" and just like that, Delta was pulled underneath the water.

"Delta!" Kira called, but there was no response. Suddenly I felt a large splash behind me followed by a terrifying screech. I turned to see something demonic. It was almost double my size and stained in blood. Bone-like spikes impaled its entire body and its arms were like long curved blades.

It swung its arm at me, but before it could hit, Flint grabbed and pushed me out the way, taking damage from the attack in my stead. He took a large gash to his back forcing him to drop his Spirit Caster into the water. We lost our only good light source. Now all that was left was moonlight that came from the sewer grates above. But even *that* was hindered from all the rain that was coming through.

I got back up and it went for another attack. I narrowly dodged each attack causing the monster to splash wildly in the water. Flint got back up with his Spirit Caster in hand and once he ignited the flames again, it got the monster's attention. The beast turned towards Flint to slice at him, but I wasn't going to let that happen again.

"Cheimerinó Fengári!" I slashed my wand up in the air causing a burst of wind to freeze half of the monster's body.

Suddenly I heard a scream coming from the other direction. It was Kira. A long arm splashed out of the water, grabbed her by the neck and raised her into the air while choking her. It looked like there was a second monster. That must have been the one that took Delta. Ranne took her sword and threw it at the beast's arm, cutting it and forcing it to let go of Kira. When she fell Ranne was right there to catch her.

The monster rose from the water. It stood on all fours and had gills all over its face. At the same time, the monster Flint and I were dealing with broke out of the ice. Flint used the fire on the end of his staff to try and stab it, but it did nothing. I couldn't tell if that meant the monster was stronger than we anticipated or if Flint was weakened, but either way we needed some room to breathe.

"Págo Toícho," I shouted, making an ice wall between us and the demon. That wasn't going to hold it for long but at least now we only had to deal with one of them.

The gilled monster lunged at us but just as it was in mid air we all heard the spell, ***"Thermosífonas!"*** Water spewed from under it like a geyser and forced it into the ceiling of the tunnel. Delta was right behind the water and shouted, "Crystal, finish it!"

I quickly ran to the pillar of water, stuck the tip of my Spirit Caster into it and said ***"Ríza Págou."*** The ice quickly spread through the water, encasing the monster inside of a thick pillar of ice.

Then we all heard a crack behind us. The first monster was breaking through the wall. It looked like this wasn't the end of the battle.

"Everyone get behind me!" Delta ordered .

"What are you going to do?" I asked.

"No time to explain! Just do it!"

We all quickly got out of Delta's way and she had a clear shot in the monster's direction. Once the monster broke through my ice wall Delta shouted, ***"Kýma!"***

All of the water in the tunnel gathered in front of her and spewed forth like a wave, flushing the monster away and out of sight.

"Ok...what the hell was that?" Kira asked, while looking over her shoulder to make sure we didn't miss one.

"I don't know," I told her. "I've never seen a creature like that in my life."

"Maybe they're the reason King Cole didn't want anyone down here." Delta suggested.

"No," Ranne corrected her. "They're here to stop us from finding the *real* reason he didn't want us down here."

"So glorified guard dogs?" Flint joked. "We must be close."

"Then let's keep moving," I told everyone.

I held the map back up as Flint held up his fire, this time much dimmer.

As we continued I asked Flint, "Are you ok?"

"I'll live," he answered. "The wound isn't that deep."

"What about your Rēa?"

"My Rēa?" he repeated.

"I can't sense it. That attack you pulled out earlier should have stopped that monster in its tracks but instead it did nothing. Are you sure you're ok?"

He paused for a moment. "I don't know. Ever since we fought the King I haven't been at full power. I was on the edge of death and I had to use every ounce of Rēa I had left to keep myself alive.

And because of that I can't feel anything. I'm at a literal fraction of my full power."

"That's kind of how I felt after we fought the Phoenix. You probably just need more rest."

"Yeah," he paused again, "probably."

Eventually we made it to the end of the tunnel and were met by a set of giant black doors. They had the design of a castle sitting on a cloud, the same exact design of the doors to the throne room back in the castle. Ranne and Flint pushed on the doors with all their might but couldn't get them to budge.

"It's locked," Ranne said. "I don't think we're gonna be able to open it."

"Move," Kira ordered as she walked up to the door and stared at it intensely.

"What is it?" Ranne asked.

"Whatever's behind this door is calling out to me."

When she said that, it reminded me of the time I first found my Spirit Caster. The entire time it called out to me until I finally found it behind a door not so different from this one. Whatever was behind this door was meant for Kira; there was no doubt about that.

Kira placed her hand on the door and as soon as she touched it, there was a loud clang from the other side. Dust started to shift as the doors opened probably for the first time in decades, if not longer. On the other side was a massive room with large columns all parallel to each other in a row leading to a large black arch. We all walked inside expecting Morpheus to be here but the place seemed empty.

"So this is supposed to be a gateway to another world?" Flint scoffed. "Seems kind of underwhelming."

Kira walked up to the large black circular archway in the center of the room and placed her hand on it. Suddenly purple flames burst from the edges and slowly made their way to the center, filling the entire arch like smoke.

"What is that?" Ranne asked, shocked at what she was seeing.

"That must be the doorway!" Delta answered.

Kira put her hand on the arch again and the energy dispersed leaving us back in the dark, quiet room .

"I take it back," Flint said. "That was kind of overwhelming."

"That energy," Kira said, "it's just like the energy I felt when I activated '*Grigoro Taxidi*'. If we go through this doorway it will lead us to somewhere entirely different."

"Well then let's go through," I told her. "For all we know Morpheus could be there right now with my sister."

"Hold on Crystal," Delta stopped me. "We have no idea what's on the other side of that portal. It could be dangerous if we all go through unprepared."

"You're exactly right, Delta," Kira agreed. "So not all of us are going through. I'll go alone to see what we're dealing with. It would be bad if we all died in there at once. I'll be putting you in charge until I come back."

"You can't go alone Kira," Ranne argued.

"This portal is calling out to me *personally*. Which means it's my duty as Queen to investigate this on my own."

"Kira, I understand why everyone shouldn't go in all at once, but you should at least take me. You lost your Spirit Caster so you're not as strong as you used to be."

"You're right. I guess I will have to have a bodyguard with me." She turned away from Ranne and looked right at me. "Crystal, will you accompany me?"

"What?" Ranne questioned. "Why *her*?"

I was just as surprised as she was. Even though Kira and I were no longer enemies, she *certainly* wasn't my ally. I could never fully forgive her for what she'd done.

"Because," Kira answered, "Crystal has a lot more at stake in this situation than any of us do. I owe it to her to let her deal with this matter alongside me. Besides, I need you and Delta to look after my kingdom while I'm away."

Ranne looked tense but she didn't say anything. She wanted to argue but instead just admitted defeat. So instead, everyone looked back at me, awaiting my answer. I looked into Kira's eyes and saw something strange. They were different from the first time we met. Not as menacing. A lot softer. The fact that she was turning into a person that I could trust was becoming more and more jarring every second I spent thinking about it.

"Yes," I answered, "I'll come with you."

"Good. Before we go we'll need a good night's rest. It's late and we'll need energy for this journey.

"But if we go back now then we might have to deal with more of those monsters again," Flint added.

"Hey guys!" Kian yelled from the other side of the room. I had completely forgotten about him. "I found a way out!"

He pointed towards a ladder that went up and out of the room.

"He's resourceful," Delta complimented.

The ladder led us out onto the streets of Ebony. Knowing exactly where the manhole was would definitely give us a fast and safe way to travel to the portal. Once we made it back to the castle we all rested, woke up at dawn and went back to the portal.

"Are you sure you don't want me to come with you?" Flint asked me. "It could be dangerous."

"It being dangerous is exactly the reason why I *don't* want you to come with me. You're still weak after our last battle. I'll be fine on my own. Just get some rest while I'm gone and I promise I'll come back as soon as possible."

"Flint," Kira interrupted. "I have a request for you."

"What is it?" he asked.

"I need you to help look after Ebony while I'm gone. You're one of the strongest Shēna here so it would be great for us if you would stay until I return."

"Well I'm not leaving Ebony until Crystal comes back, so why not? I think it will be a good way to kill time."

"Thank you."

Kira put her hand on the arch turning on the portal. She looked back at me and asked, "Are you ready?"

"Yeah, I'm ready," I answered. We both took a step through the portal with clasped hands. We had no idea what would be awaiting us and that scared me. But it didn't matter how scared I was. If it meant saving my sister, I would dive down into the depths of hell and fight through the flames if it came to it.

CHAPTER THIRTEEN
ALIZEH

I woke up laying in the sand with the rising sun beaming in my eyes. To my left and right were ruins of an unfamiliar town long deserted. The worst part about all this was that my body was bound by chains so I couldn't move enough to stand or even push myself up. And I couldn't remember how I got into this situation until I tilted my head up to see Arachne and the man who beat me from before. I shimmied my hand over to my holster but couldn't feel my Spirit Caster, then looked up again and saw that the man was holding my Spirit Caster in his hand.

"Don't struggle," he told me. "You'll only wear yourself out."

I glared at him and asked, "What are you going to do with me?"

"Nothing," Arachne answered, "so long as you cooperate with us."

"Cooperate with you? You poisoned my mother and kidnapped my father! When I get out of this I'm going to *kill* you!"

"I think you have me confused with someone else. I don't even know who you are, kid."

"Don't play dumb with me Arachne! I know you did it!"

She looked taken aback from my outburst and removed her hood making it easier for me to see her face. There was something different about it but I couldn't put my finger on what exactly. It seemed slimmer.

"Did you just now say Arachne?" She asked. "That's my sister's name."

That's when it finally clicked.

"Are you... Arachne's twin?" I asked.

"Yes, I am."

I slammed the back of my head into the sand and said, "Well that's embarrassing. Sorry about trying to kill you."

"Don't worry, I get it a lot. But if you really want to atone then you're going to have to tell me where my sister is."

"Sorry but I can't help you. Like I said before, she's done some unforgivable things to me. I've been looking for her too and so far I've got no clue where she is. Why are *you* looking for her?"

"Because I think she's in trouble. She's been dealing with Morpheus and he's no good for her. Especially with everything he's planning. They could shake the entire fabric of our reality if they aren't stopped soon."

That piqued my interest. It reminded me of when Arachne once told me that she was meant for 'so much more' than what her current position in life was. She claimed that she would steal the throne. Maybe she meant something more by that statement.

"What is he planning?" I asked.

"He's trying to become a god." That was the last thing I was expecting her to say. I couldn't even wrap my head around what that even meant. She could probably tell because right after she continued saying, "Look, there's a lot more to his plan that would take too long to fully explain, so I'm going to sum it up to the parts that are important to you. Morpheus is going to a temple that was built on grounds that have a potent amount of Rēa infused into them and the surrounding area. Morpheus will then use that Rēa to perform a spell that will require human sacrifices to make himself more powerful than any one Shēna can handle."

I leaned myself up and shouted, "Wait, did you just say human sacrifices? That's probably why he took my father! Why are we just sitting here? We have to go find him, now!"

"Because there's a problem with that. There are two temples we know of that he could be going to, but we have no idea which one it'll be."

"Where are the temples?"

"Neró City and Nótio Págo."

"Woah, Neró City is like, super far from the Black Continent! Alright, you guys can take the city. I'll go to Nótio Págo. I need to head in that direction anyway to give my mother the cure for the poison your sister forced in her."

After saying that I realized something. I looked around and didn't see my bag anywhere. It looked like I had left it all the way back in town. The plant was still inside of it!

Then the man who had been silent for our entire conversation finally spoke, "Looking for this?" He held up my bag! "I thought that whatever was in it might've been important so I decided to take it along with us."

Next thing I knew, the chains that had once bound me suddenly dispersed into Rēa. The chains must've been a part of his spell. Once I was free he tossed my bag over to me and said, "Let's divide and conquer."

"Wait!" The woman said, "I don't think sending out a little girl to fight Morpheus and my sister is a good idea. Especially if she's going alone."

Once again there was another adult who insisted on patronizing me.

"Hey I've fought them before," I told her. "And I was able to beat your sister once already. I can easily do it again."

The woman looked shocked and said, "There's no way you've beaten her before!"

"Don't worry," the man cut in saying, "she's telling the truth. This girl's strong. I can beat her any day of the week if she performed the same way she did in our last battle... but it would be a completely different story if she actually would've gone all out."

This man was perceptive. He could tell I was holding back for the majority of our battle. But I could tell he was holding back too.

"Thank you," I told him before turning to the woman and saying, "And thank you too for the information... oh wait. I just realized. I don't know your names."

"Mercury Argyris," the man said.

"Amethyst Isley," the woman told me.

"Alizeh Green," I smiled back. "I hope we meet again."

"Our goals are the same, which means our fates are connected. We'll meet again eventually," Mercury pointed out.

I nodded my head and said, ***"Paírno Ptísi."*** It forced me into the air and I was off to Livádia. After hours of flying I finally made it back to my mothers doctor and gave him the plant.

"Is this the right one?"

"It is!" The doctor said in shock. "We'll turn this into medicine for your mother right away."

I sighed from relief. My mother was going to be saved. But there wasn't any time to rest. Now there was a new threat looming over me; my father was going to be used for some crazy sacrifice. I was tired but I had to keep going. My next stop was going to be Nótio Págo.

CHAPTER FOURTEEN
RAI

"Wake up Aeson, it's dawn."

He was startled awake by my words.

"Your mother made you breakfast. If you take too long to eat then I'm leaving without you."

He jumped out of bed and ran around his room frantically to get ready and I left him to it. Once I walked through the living room I passed his mother saying, "Tell him I'll be outside waiting for him."

She grabbed my wrist, stopping me, "Hey, make sure you bring him back *alive.*"

"Don't worry," I told her, "I will."

"Aeson is a good child. He's polite, he listens but ... he's not exactly someone you would classify as a hero. He's not a fighter. He can give you support, but I think when it comes down to it he won't be able to handle this lifestyle."

"Good to know. By the time he's done with this journey, that'll change."

I walked out of the house and waited on the steps for a while before finally deciding that I was tired of waiting. *He'll catch up,* I thought to myself. As I started walking on the path I heard him yell my name.

"Rai, wait for me!" Aeson shouted with his large backpack and heavy clothes. As soon as he caught up to me he huffed and puffed while holding his knees.

"Are you already out of breath?" I asked. "We're not even a full minute away from your house."

"Sorry I'm not really good at running."

"Well that will have to change. Shēna have to travel around the world during their adventures. If your stamina's that low then you won't be any help to anyone. So to bring up that stamina, we'll be running from here to Nótio Págo without pause."

"What? But we'll be running for days..."

"Then I guess we'll just have to start now."

I turned and took off. Aeson looked shocked before trying to run after me. I obviously wasn't going to make him run for days without pause but I thought it would be hilarious to make him think that. To my surprise he actually started to keep up with me. Tears streamed down his face as he did, so it was definitely a struggle for him, but even so, I could feel something awaken in him. Rēa. That's what he was using to keep up with me. It didn't even look like he meant to use it. I wasn't at all going my top speed but that still spoke volumes on his true potential.

"You actually seem serious about this," I told him as we ran.

"Yes ma'am," he struggled to say. "I need to bring my brother back. I don't think he's safe with those people."

"There are a couple things you need to know. First off, don't ever call me *ma'am* again. That was disgusting."

"Sorry, Sir?"

"It's just Rai."

"Oh, ok. Sorry Rai."

"The second thing I need to bring up… And I know your mother probably told you this already but this is going to be dangerous. I can try to keep you out of harm's way, but there's only so much I can do. You might even die on this trip. Aren't you scared of that?"

"The thought terrifies me. But I know there are Shēna out there like you and my mother, willing to put their lives on the line in situations like this. I want to be like that. I want to *experience* that."

That made me stop and laugh out loud. He stopped right along with me to take a breath and ask, "What's so funny?"

"Nothing," I told him, "you just remind me of someone."

"Remind you of who?"

"This girl I know. Another Shēna who I think is just a year older than you are. She has a pretty similar reason for why she goes on these types of adventures. Except she's more in it for the fun."

That seemed to peak his interest because right after I said that he asked, "We're almost the same age? What's her name?"

"Alizeh." I told him. "She's one of the people who helped me defeat the King."

"Wait, a girl my age helped you defeat King Cole?"

"Along with a few others, yeah."

"How'd you do it?"

"It's a long story."

"We have time before we reach Nótio Págo. I'd be really happy if you told it to me on the way."

"Fine kid, if you insist. But first get on my back."

"Oh there's no need for that. I don't mind running *too* much."

"I understand that, but if you get on it'll be a lot faster, and time is of the essence," I told him while kneeling down.

"Ok, if you say so," he said while climbing on.

"Hold on tight. If you fall off I'm not coming back for you."

"Don't worry, I think I'll be able to—"

"Víma Flas,"

Electricity surrounded our bodies and after my first step we took off, going faster than he could comprehend. I thought that he'd probably get nauseous after this run but I couldn't take it into consideration. Like I said before, time was of the essence.

CHAPTER FIFTEEN
CRYSTAL

The purple flames didn't burn. I could only feel warmth on my skin as I brushed past waves like thick flowing leaves. When I opened my eyes again I saw that we were in another large room that paralleled the previous one when it came to its architecture. But there was a massively noticeable difference. The entire room was coated in gold and the structure of the walls, pillars and tiles were in much better condition than the room on the other side of the portal.

"What is this place?" I asked. "The portal obviously took us somewhere different but is this really another world? It doesn't look too dissimilar from our own."

"I don't know," Kira answered. "But something feels familiar about it."

"Familiar how?" I questioned.

"It's the air here. It feels thick. *Heavy*. Not like our own. But I've felt it before when I traveled through Grígoro Taxídi."

"I feel it too. Maybe it's an after effect from going through the portal."

"No," she corrected me. "There was never an after effect when I used the spell."

"Well then what are you trying to say?"

"I've been here before. Every time I walked through my old portal spell and travelled through that black desert, I was entering this dimension."

"Well does this room look familiar?"

"No, I've never seen any signs of civilization when I went through my own portal. Just a wasteland. So whatever it is we just stepped into ... It's all new to me."

"Then I guess we better start exploring. There are doors over there. Let's see where they lead."

We went over to the doors, pushed them open, and walked through, but we were greeted by two knights in shining black armor. They were both just as surprised to see us as we were of them.

"Intruders," one of the men shuddered. They both drew their weapons. At first I thought they were normal swords until the edges of the blade started to burn bright as if it were just taken out of a forge. Even odder was the color of the hot metal. It was a brilliant fiery blue that looked like it could've only been made with magic. But I didn't feel an ounce of Rēa coming from any of these men. But those weapons ... They were different.

I put my hand on my hip, grazing my Spirit Caster just in case things were to escalate.

"Wait," Kira put her arms out in immediate surrender, "we don't mean you any harm."

"If so then turn back now!" the soldier barked at us. "Or we *will* be forced to take lethal action."

They both came in close with a nervous look in their eyes. They were scared of us but still willing to put up a fight. A dangerous combination. The kind that would make a man swing first and ask questions later.

"I'm sorry but we can't do that," I told them without taking my eyes off of there's. I already decided that we passed the point of no return and I wasn't turning back.

Kira looked at me with the same old hatred that she used to. She obviously wanted to de-escalate the situation but I didn't see that happening. Especially once they both took another step towards us, tensing up as they were both ready to swing. It was either us or them.

I pulled out my Spirit Caster while pushing Kira out of the way and yelled, ***"Cheimerinó Fengári!"***

A large burst of energy made them fly back and forced one of them to freeze to the wall. The other one sat in shock and simply said, "A-a Shēna!" He quickly got up and ran to the other wall, slamming his fist down on a button and yelled, **"Intruder alert! A Shēna has entered through the portal! I repeat!"**

His words boomed and echoed through the halls. I didn't know how but he was alerting everyone here of our presence. I uttered the same spell from before and used it to freeze this man too.

"You're really not helping our situation right now," Kira growled.

"They were going to attack us."

"You don't know that!"

"Well I have you to thank for teaching me to never take my chances."

She wanted to argue but she knew she couldn't refute *that* specific fact, so she bit her tongue.

"We need to get out of here," I told her. "This place will be swarming with guards."

I rushed through the next set of doors and found myself in a tunnel that went left and right.

"The room that we came through was a mirror image of the one in our world, but this tunnel is a completely different layout," Kira pointed out. "Escape might not be so easy."

"Then we'll just have to follow our instincts and hope for the best. Let's go."

We ran through the golden halls and heard what sounded like a stampede not too far behind. And far up ahead could be seen a whole group of soldiers, turning around the corner.

"It's the intruders!" one shouted.

"Don't let them escape!" another ordered with their magical weapon drawn.

"Damnit," I cursed under my breath while readying for another attack, "they couldn't of made this easy?"

Kira stopped me and tugged on my collar, pulling me up a set of stairs that I overlooked. I almost tripped up the stairs but quickly got my footing before smacking her hand off me.

"Don't drag me along like I'm some sort of child!" I snapped at her.

"Then stop acting like one! Just because you beat my father doesn't mean you're the strongest. We have no idea what we're dealing with."

We ran up the stairs and once we finally got to the top I was shocked at what I saw. We were in some type of golden city. The sky was dark but filled with so much color. Gigantic blue, pink, and white clouds filled the sky while stars of every color of the rainbow shined brightly lighting everything up. The strangest part of it was the fact that the sun was out as if it were still day.

"What is this?" Kira asked.

"I don't know. It looks like the southern lights back in Nótio Págo."

No. That was wrong. The southern lights couldn't be compared to what I was looking at. This was magical.

"Look out!" Kira shouted before pushing me to the ground. Once I fell, I saw something fly right into Kira forcing her to the ground with me.

I quickly got back up while shouting, "Kira!" And saw that something had burnt right through the back of her dress, charring her right shoulder. She was going to live but I didn't understand what could have hurt her like that. It was like a dangerous spell.

I looked up and scanned the area spotting a blue glint of light at the top of a nearby tower. Right before I could fully comprehend what I was looking at, it shot itself towards me like a falling star. I just narrowly dodged it and watched as it burnt a small hole in the ground.

I looked back up and saw a person at the top of the tower holding a weapon of some sort that started to glow just like before. And it wasn't just them. Every tower in the area had a soldier pointing the same weapon that was ready to fire away.

As they blasted their attacks off I shouted, ***"Págo Toícho,"*** forcing a wall of ice to block the projectiles. But the attacks seemed endless and my ice wall wasn't going to last forever. We needed more cover in order to escape.

I started my first incantation.

"Let the ice rain down."

As I spoke the soldiers who were following us from before were rushing out of the stairwell that we had just come from. This was starting to become more than I could handle.

"Blind my enemies to death."
"Take them off their course"
"Cheimoniátiki Kataigída"

Right before they could grab Kira and I, the soldiers were blown away from the bursting wind that emitted from us. Frosty clouds of ice shrouded the area making it hard for anyone to see us.

"Can you stand?" I asked while she was already pushing herself off the floor.

"Yeah," she grunted. "Only thing hard to move is my arm."

I grabbed her by her other arm and said, "Good enough. Right now, we need to move!"

We ran through the small, artificial storm cloud until we finally reached the inner parts of the city. Everything was metallic. The buildings were golden, the streets were like obsidian, and even the lanterns were brighter. They were so golden that I couldn't see the flames inside, that is if there were any. Even the people were gold. Not their skin per se, but the ones I glanced at as we ran by had golden silk robes. We definitely didn't fit in and just our mere presence alone was enough to draw attention.

As we ran through the streets another soldier clad in black armor everywhere but his face ran from around the corner and shouted at us, "Halt! You two are under arrest! Surrender now or I will be forced to—"

I didn't let him finish. With my Spirit Caster still in hand I shouted over him, ***"Cheimerinó Fengári!"*** Ice spewed forth and froze him right in his place.

Everyone in the area who once gawked at us was now screaming in terror and scattered away with the belief that they might have been next. We had to follow suit. Sticking around in one place for too long was likely a death sentence. We needed to find somewhere secluded.

Once we ran past the frozen soldier, I heard the ice shatter.

Kira and I immediately stopped in our tracks. Not simply out of curiosity but from instinctual fear. We looked back at the soldier to see that he had completely broken out of the ice. And somehow he looked completely different. The dark skinned man had long black locks and brown eyes before. But this time his eyes were crimson and his hair was as white as mine. And oddly enough somehow his clear face was now stained with white tribal tattoos. This sudden change combined with the fact that he broke out of my ice so effortlessly meant that this man was no normal human.

"A Zubarian?" I guessed aloud, hoping that Kira would have an answer.

"Those eyes are familiar but the rest of him isn't. I've never seen a Zubarian transform like this."

If he was anything like Barin or Ana then we probably weren't going to be able to escape. We had to fight and then move on. I readied myself thinking of a spell that could take him down quickly, but before I could say another word he ran at me and within a blink of an eye he was already behind me. I wasn't his target.

I looked over at Kira to see him landing his fist right into her stomach bringing her to her knees without even the sound of a yelp to accompany it.

"Cheimerinó—" I started to say while winding up my wand, but before I could swing it he hit me right in my face, forcing me to fly across the street, smash through a window and crash through a table or two before I could finally hit the ground. Never in my life had I felt an impact like that. And I couldn't even tell if it was a punch or a kick. All I knew was that it took me out of commission.

CHAPTER SIXTEEN
KIRA

I wasn't ready for the attack. I didn't even see him coming. And Crystal was in an even worse position. I couldn't even tell if she was alive. I on the other hand could barely breathe. And for a moment, when I thought I caught my breath... I ended up expelling everything from my body. Breakfast from this morning, my lunch from yesterday and ... maybe even a little bit of blood? I couldn't tell. It felt like I was going to die. Just from a simple punch.

"Crystal?" I was able to cough out. "Crystal!"

There was no answer. I couldn't see her anymore. She had been smashed through what seemed to be a shop of some sorts on the street corner. And she wasn't getting back up. She truly was out for the count. Hell, *I* was out for the count.

The soldier grabbed me by my injured arm forcing me to gasp in pain and then forced shackles on me that were more mechanical than I had ever seen. They tightened around my wrists while other soldiers finally came to swarm the area.

"This one's already subdued. The other one is incapacitated in that restaurant over there. Cuff her and bring her in," The soldier ordered while his hair, eyes and face went back to normal.

I finally caught my breath and had to find a way to talk my way out of this. It was the only thing I was capable of doing.

"Wait!" I shouted, while still coughing. "This is unjustified! We mean you no harm and haven't done anything to provoke a valid arrest."

"As soon as you arrived in this dimension, you attacked my men. And attempted to evade authorities."

"That was in self defense!"

But he didn't care. He just pushed me into the other soldiers and ordered, "Put her in a cell,"

They grabbed me and pulled on my injured arm, forcing me to shriek out a grumbled scream. "I will not stand for this! I am Kira Black, Queen of the Black Continent! I will not have you imprison me like some lowly commoner!"

"Quiet down!" one of the soldiers shouted while trying to pull me away.

"Wait," their leader ordered. "Did you just say that you were the Queen of the Black Continent?"

The recognition shocked me, but I didn't want it to show.

"Oh, so it seems like my reputation *does* stretch out this far. Even into different dimensions," I grinned, desperately trying to regain my composure.

"Where is your Spirit Caster?" he asked me.

"I no longer have one. It was recently destroyed in battle."

The knight simply just glared at me before turning to another and saying, "Tell the Cosmic Queen that the new Black Continent ruler has entered her dimension. Lock these two up until she gives us further orders."

CHAPTER SEVENTEEN
FLINT

I stood next to the closed portal with Ranne by my side doing the same, but obviously for different reasons.

"You must really care about her," I guessed. "Kira, I mean."

"Of course I do. She is the Queen of the Black Continent and I've sworn to protect her. It's my *job* to care."

I laughed at that and said, "Yeah I guess you've got an excuse."

I kept staring at the arch, desperately wishing that it would open back up.

"I should have gone with them," I said.

"You're worried about Crystal?" Ranne asked with a raised brow.

"Yeah. I have no idea where that portal took her and there's no way for me to go through it if she needs me. Last time she needed me," I paused for a moment reminiscing of the first time we met, "when she *really* needed me I was there to help." I walked away from the portal and slid down a nearby piller to take a seat. "When all of this first started I didn't want any part of it. But even though she's so damn serious all the time she was still able to draw me in.

She is charismatic in a way I can't fully comprehend. But I guess I can't blame that all on her. She's got some pretty suggestive friends. What she pulled off was suicide, but she didn't do it alone. I was there. Her friends too. I can't be there for her this time. None of us can."

Ranne turned back to the arch and said, "I wouldn't worry about Crystal if I were you. She beat Morpheus in battle. And she pushed Kira and the former King to their absolute limits. I met Crystal before she ever used magic. That day I saw a scared desperate child who couldn't even help her own family. Now I see a dangerous being who will stop at nothing to achieve her goals. The look in her eyes... they changed to something unrecognizable. You should trust in her abilities."

"You say that and yet you're sitting here just as worried as I am."

"I'm worried because Kira is not the same as Crystal. Her Spirit Caster was completely destroyed and now she's powerless. Ten days ago she had the power to level a city and now she can't even defend herself. She's basically human now."

"Well that shouldn't matter too much," I told her. "She's with Crystal."

"And you really think Crystal will protect her? Let's not forget that just last week, they were at each other's necks."

"I think Crystal's actions were more than justified."

"I agree. And *that's* what scares me. They're all alone in there. At any moment Crystal could just snap, and just like that I could lose Kira forever."

As much as I didn't want to believe it, it was a valid possibility. I doubt that Crystal would be over the situation but now isn't the time to fight. She needed Kira to help her find her sister. I could only hope that she would remember that fact.

Delta cleared her throat, catching our attention. She was sitting on the far side of the room while leaning against a pillar and said, "I think it's time we get out of here. We've been cooped up here for long enough. Ebony needs guidance and we need to give it to them. Kira and Crystal wouldn't want us wasting our time like this."

"Yeah, you're right," Ranne agreed as she started walking towards her. I looked back at the portal before agreeing. I needed to be patient and trust her, so I left with them to go back to the castle.

***

I sat atop the stone wall of the castle and looked out at the city. The destruction reminded me of Phoenix Island. I needed to get back to it. This war seemed to be over, so it was time to rebuild. I decided that as soon as I knew that Crystal was safe I would leave. But for now I would help with what I could.

Before I got up I overheard someone below say, "Where is the Queen?"

I looked down and saw a large group of people, Knights and commoners alike all talking in the courtyard.

"I don't know," someone answered. "She just keeps disappearing from everyone's sight."

"I haven't seen her at all."

"To think that in our time of need, our own Queen is nowhere to be found. What kind of leader is she?"

"Her entire bloodline is corrupt," someone added. "I wouldn't put it past her to just abandon us until we sort out this mess ourselves."

A woman spoke saying, "You know what I've heard?"

"What have you heard?"

"Rumor has it that Queen Kira was the one who caused all of this destruction. People saw her turn into some hideous beast with her magic and cause all this madness."

These were all words that could spark a revolt. It would serve Kira right for what she's done to my home, but at the same time it would cause too much chaos in a place already filled with it. These people don't deserve to go through that. I had to warn Delta.

CHAPTER EIGHTEEN
KIRA

◯

I sat on the bench in the empty cell trying my best to not fall out of it from my spinning head. A pool of blood sat in the corner after I barfed it all out from the nausea. I've been feeling dizzy ever since that soldier hit me. That with the fact that my shoulder was still in pain from getting shot by that strange energy, made it hard for me to sit still and stay calm. To keep myself from passing out, I constantly tapped my foot on the metallic floor while wondering when or *if* they were going to bring Crystal to the same cell as me. I didn't even know if she was still alive. If he would have hit me with that kick then I would have surely died. But Crystal still had her Spirit Caster. She could have shielded herself with Rēa but regardless she was still caught off guard.

Soon the sound of metal clanging came closer and closer until finally on the other side of the bars I could see the man who was responsible for our capture.

"Kira Black," the soldier called while opening the sliding metal bars. "Queen Céleste has ordered an audience with you."

I stood up straight and carried myself the way any royal would while saying, "Well I'm glad we're on the same page." I walked with him out of the cell, trying my best not to fall over with my hands still bound together while being surrounded by guards. So this is what it felt like to not be the one in control.

As we walked, I asked, "Where's the woman I came here with?"

He looked over at me with tired eyes debating if he should give me any information at all. But surprisingly enough he still answered, "She's currently in the infirmary."

"Is she ok?"

"I wouldn't know," he looked forward. "She never woke up during our transport. But I didn't hit her that hard, so she'll probably live."

"You smashed her through a window," I argued.

"I could've taken her head off if I wanted to. You both got off easy. You're lucky I didn't feel like killing a bunch of spoiled brats."

I could tell that he was being serious. The fact that I wasn't in the same state as Crystal proved that he was holding back. The soldiers of this world have a lot more integrity than the ones in mine.

We walked for ages until finally reaching the throne room doors that looked similar to my own.

Once they opened the door I was confused at who, or rather *what* I was looking at. They walked me in front of the throne and I couldn't even comprehend if what I saw was even a human.

Its body seemed like that of a woman. She wore no clothes but she didn't seem naked. Her skin was just a black void like the night sky, but it was moving. Small bright dots swirled around her skin like shooting stars. Her eyes were like portals and her hair was large, fluffy and flowing, not fully like an afro but more like a thundercloud.

"There's no doubt about it," her voice echoed. ***"You truly are Cole's daughter."***

Her words shocked me. She knew my father. And even more shocking was the fact that she could tell from just one look.

I stopped my gawking and asked, "How could you tell?"

"I could feel it," she answered. ***"Your spirit reeks of his stench. I could tell as soon as you entered my world. If you wanted an audience with me why didn't you just show my knights your Spirit Caster? They would have noticed it right away."***

It took me a moment to come up with an answer after still being in awe of her appearance. Her entire body looked like the embodiment of the night sky that laid upon this dimension. "I ... no longer have it," I told her. "It was destroyed in battle not too long ago."

"I see. Well if that's the case then why did you come here? Certainly you didn't think you could beat me without your most powerful weapon."

"I didn't come here to fight."

"That's the only thing that you people come here for. If not to expand your territory, then what other reason would there be?"

"Because I owed someone a favor. Crystal Winters; the girl that I came here with. She's looking for her sister. A young girl who was kidnapped by a man named Morpheus Morningstar. All the evidence he left behind pointed in this direction so we thought he might be here."

"Well I can assure you he's not. I would have noticed."

"Is that so? Well, I guess I'll have to take your word for it. I apologize for disturbing the peace, and I humbly ask for forgiveness. I'm still needed back in my world so if you could pardon me and my friend then I would be eternally grateful."

She stared at me with a perplexed look before asking, ***"Are you serious? That's all you wanted?"*** The air of mystery and divinity around her disappeared and was replaced by something much more ... human.

"Yes. I'm sorry if I have inconvenienced you in any way from our trespassing."

She stood up and said, ***"You're different from the ones who have come before you,"*** then her body disappeared for a split second before reappearing right in front of me, making me jump. She caressed my face to calm me and said, ***"Don't move,"*** before placing her forehead right next to mine.

In the next moment I could see my entire life flash before my eyes. The childhood that I spent with Ranne. The loving touch of my mother. The mental abuse from my father. I saw everything. But the things that stuck out the most were the memories with Crystal. The time I killed her parents up until the time she killed mine.

Once it was over I fell to the floor in shock.

"W-what did you do to me?" I shouted.

"I read your mind and your intentions."

"What are you?"

"The creator of worlds. Master of Space. I am who I am just as you are who you are." She stretched out her hand to help me up and I took it. *"I can sense that you are no longer the person that you used to be. No longer the scum that your ancestors were. Kira, you have broken that cycle of hatred."*

"Does it really matter? I've broken it far too late and I've hurt too many people to be redeemed. I was never meant to wield a Spirit Caster." I said as I turned away from her.

"That's a lie. All of my children were meant to have this power."

"Your *'children'*?"

"Of course. I see all Shēna as my children, since your power originated from me. And I still believe that you deserve said power. Tell me Kira, if you got your power back, what would you do with it?"

Learning that the source of my power came from this being shook me. I had never known the origins of Rēa. I wondered if it was really true, but that was a question for another time.

"If I got my power back," I answered, "then I would use it to help everyone. My entire kingdom. I don't want to hurt anyone ever again."

"I like that answer," she smiled. *"Alright then, it's time to get you a new Spirit Caster."*

***

The soldier pulled out a key that instantly eased the pressure on my large shackles, causing them to fall to the floor.

"Finally," I said while rubbing my wrist. "They were beginning to chafe."

"Aleron," the Queen spoke to the soldier. ***"I need you to personally escort Kira to Abraham so he can give her a new Spirit Caster. But knowing him he should already be expecting her."***

I didn't know how a man I've never met would be expecting me. The only possibility would be that he was told of my arrival beforehand but that wouldn't make any sense. This arrangement was only made seconds ago. And before I was simply just a lowly criminal to this world. I doubted her statement but if it were true then I was going to meet yet another supernatural being that I probably wasn't going to be able to comprehend.

"But before you take her there," the Queen continued, ***"I want you to first take her to the infirmary to get treated by Ziva personally. I feel a disturbance in the flow of her Rēa. If it isn't corrected soon, it could have fatal consequences in the near future."***

"Right away my Queen," he bowed before turning my way. "Come with me."

I followed him out of the throne room and asked him, "Aleron was it? Tell me, who is this *Ziva*? Is she some kind of doctor?"

"Yeah," he answered while still looking forward. "She's our best healer."

"Is that so? I'm hoping that means my friend is under their care."

"I wouldn't be able to say for sure. She's a very busy woman and that girl probably isn't the highest priority on her list. But if any one can tell you her whereabouts and condition, then it's going to be Ziva."

We turned a corner that was different from the one we came from and walked until we reached the end of the hall. It was a dead end; becoming a raised metallic platform engraved in ruins I had never seen before.

"What's this?" I asked. "Some kind of secret passageway?"

"Yeah, something like that," he half answered while clicking a slew of buttons attached to the pedestal that protruded from the platform.

Once he clicked the final button the runes on the floor started to glow blue and for the sharpest second I felt Rēa building up beneath my feet. Before I could react there was a flash of light that enveloped us. Even though I flinched, it didn't hurt. But it did disorient me. The location looked entirely different. We were still in a hallway but the walls and floor were perfectly white. And the ceiling had a bright glow to it that lit up the entire hall.

"What just happened?" I asked, taking longer than I should've to observe my surroundings. "Where are we?"

"We just now teleported from the castle to the hospital," he told me as he continued walking.

"But that was instant," I lagged behind. "My portals have never taken me anywhere that fast."

"Well our teleportation is far superior than whatever spells you have in your world. The Queen put her own energy into fueling Abraham's machine. "

"Abraham? You mean the man you're supposed to be taking me too made that thing?"

He simply grunted and nodded his head. Abraham must've been a genius. Far smarter than anyone in our dimension. It was no wonder why I couldn't comprehend anything in the Skoteinós Kósmos. Their technological advancements were centuries ahead of ours.

I followed him out of the hall, passing up a slew of men and women, all wearing white; all busy with saving lives. But there was a neatness to them.

Aleron soon brought me into a room with a large table in the center of it. Two people sat in front of a large window that didn't lead outside, but to another room. And in that room laying alone on a bed at its center was none other than Crystal.

"Well would you look at that," Aleron nudged me. "Looks like she *is* treating your friend." A statement that put me at ease. He then said aloud, "Ziva, the Queen has requested for you personally to do a medical check on this girl here."

Ziva swiveled her chair around to get a good look at me. She was old. Yet had youthful eyes. Her skin was dark and her hair was long and black, similar to my own.

She slowly got out of her seat while saying, "Well if the Queen is personally asking for *me* to see this girl, then she must be special." As she walked over to me she turned back to the other much younger woman who was sitting beside her and said, "Haoma, can you take care of the scans for that patient?"

Haoma was obviously caught off guard by the request and was ever so slightly flustered but still agreed to the command.

"Yes ma'am," she said as she turned away back to the machines.

As Ziva walked up to me, she asked, "And what might your name be young lady?"

Regardless of how in awe I still was of my entire situation, I remembered to stand tall and answer with as much regal dignity as I could muster.

"My name is Kira Black, and I am the Queen of the Black Continent."

Her eyes widened as she looked over to Aleron and said, "Oh dear Aleron, you never announced that I was in the presence of royalty."

She then bowed, bringing herself all the way to her knees. "Forgive me Queen Kira." She was the first person here to actually respect my title. It felt good. But seeing the elderly grovel in such an uncomfortable position wasn't something that helped me relish the situation.

"You may rise," I ordered.

Once she got back to her feet she said, "Allow me to introduce myself. My name is Ziva Aceso and I am the Chief Medical officer of Kitrinose. What seems to be the problem?"

"I'm not exactly sure," I told her. "Ever since the General over here hit me in the stomach, the pain hasn't really gone away. And I've been feeling nauseous ever since."

Ziva raised an eyebrow at Aleron while asking, "You struck the Queen?"

"She was an unannounced intruder and a momentary threat to Queen Céleste along with the other girl you're currently caring for," he explained callously.

Ziva looked back at me, "And you said that this all started right after Aleron struck you in the abdomen?"

"Yes, ever since then it's just been constant pain," I told her while holding my stomach grimacing from the injury. Ok, perhaps I may have been overselling the injury but seeing that ass of a General get chewed out was definitely the most entertaining thing to witness since I entered the dimension.

He rolled his eyes seeing right through my charade while scoffing under his breath. And in return she scowled at him.

"Why didn't you bring her here immediately after her arrest along with the other girl?" she nagged. "She's obviously suffering from some internal bleeding! It's a miracle she's still standing."

"Ms. Aceso," Haoma interrupted, "the scans are complete."

She pushed a button causing an apparition of some sort to appear above the table. It was a human skeleton with bright red markings all around its skull.

"What is that?" I asked while taking a few steps back.

"An X-ray of your friend's skeleton. This hologram helps us see exactly what's out of place and what needs to be fixed."

"Besides the many abrasions we already found, the main two injuries seem to be from her concussion and dislocated jaw," Haoma explained.

"Nothing I can't fix," Ziva claimed with confidence. "Kira, if you don't mind, I'd like to mend both of your wounds at the same time. Wouldn't want one of you dying while I fix the other."

"Of course," I nodded, "that would be greatly appreciated if it's not too much trouble."

"Excellent. Come with me."

CHAPTER NINETEEN
CRYSTAL

The last thing I remembered was gathering as much Rēa around my body as I could muster before taking a destructive attack right to my face. I was out almost instantly and now all I could feel was an intense pain around my jaw and head. But bit by bit the feeling started to ease up until something finally *popped*.

I was jolted awake but I couldn't move. My wrist and ankles were tied to a bed in the center of a white room. To my right was an old lady with a Spirit Caster muttering some kind of incantation.

"Who are you?" I asked.

But her eyes were closed as she said the incantation. I didn't know her intentions, and I wasn't going to sit back when there was a chance I was in some serious danger.

"What are you doing?" I shouted as I struggled to break free from my binds.

"Crystal, please shut up."

I looked over to my left to see Kira sitting beside my bed, completely unfazed by the current situation. And unlike myself, she wasn't restrained.

"Kira?" I asked, starting to realize that maybe I wasn't in as much danger as I had originally thought.

"She's making sure we don't die, so please calm down," Kira sighed.

I was still confused about our current situation, but seeing Kira at ease made me want to do the same. And it wasn't hard after feeling warm energy travel through my head. The pressure in my head decreased more and more until I finally felt nothing.

"Alright," the old woman said as she got up to undo my bonds. "That should stop the bleeding and fix any broken bones. I highly suggest that you both go and see Tallulah so you can replenish any lost blood. Especially you Kira."

"Can that wait?" Kira asked while standing from her seat. "I have some important business I need to attend to within this dimension."

"Of course. But I wouldn't wait any longer than a day." The older lady continued as she finished undoing my bonds. "You're free to go."

"Um, thank you." I said, still not fully understanding what was going on but knowing that it was probably a good thing.

Kira made her way to the door while saying, "Come on Crystal. There's something I need to take care of."

I quickly jumped off the bed and followed behind her while asking, "Who was that woman? Did she just heal us?"

"Her name is Ziva. And yeah, she's the highest ranking medical officer in this dimension."

We walked through a door that opened on its own once we approached it and closed after we passed. That alone seemed like magic, but Kira was unfazed by it. I could barely take my eyes off of it, and once I did, I turned to see a not so friendly face. It was the same man who knocked me out and put me in this disorienting situation.

I reached for my hip to grab my Spirit Caster but my holster was empty. They must've confiscated it after my arrest.

Kira looked back at me and asked, "What's wrong?" Before immediately taking a double take back at the man and then back at me. "Oh you don't have to worry about his mean mug. He knows I'm royalty so he's not going to hurt us again."

That was the moment where I could no longer take being in the dark.

"What the hell happened while I was out?" I asked.

"A lot of diplomacy," she smirked. "I'll explain it all on the walk." She then turned back to the soldier and ordered, "Aleron, take me to Abraham."

***

Before we left, I collected my Spirit Caster and followed them through the teleporter, which was disorienting to say the least. It didn't take long after for Kira to give me the basics of our situation but there was only one thing that I cared about.

"So the Queen of this dimension is absolutely sure that my sister isn't here?" I asked.

"Yeah she's pretty sure," Kira confirmed. "And she was able to specifically sense me as soon as I stepped foot in this dimension, so I believe she has some sort of ability or heightened awareness that helps her keep track of everyone in this world. I'd take her assumption as fact."

"Ok but just because Morpheus and Arachne aren't here now doesn't mean they won't be here in the future. I mean this place is their whole goal, right? They'll have to show up sooner or later."

"My thoughts exactly. I say we wait here for a while. There's no need for us to leave just yet since this place is our only lead. Besides, I have some business to take care of anyway so that only works in my favor."

"Oh yeah, I totally forgot you mentioned that before. What exactly is that business? And where is this guy taking us?"

"I have a name you know," the soldier growled while looking over his shoulder and back at me. "And it's rude to talk about someone as if they're not in the same space as you, damn brat."

"Oh sorry," I gulped, "I just didn't know your name."

"Well I guess now's as good a time as any for introductions," Kira suggested.

The man rolled his eyes while saying, "Very well. My name is Aleron Chevalier and I am the General of this kingdom's army."

"Kira Black, Queen of the Black Continent. But you already knew that."

"I'm Crystal Winters, but you can just call me Crystal. I don't have any fancy titles like you two."

"Alright Crystal, to answer your question from before, I've been personally ordered by Queen Céleste to take you both to Abraham's Forge."

"And why are we going there?"

"To get your Queen a new Spirit Caster."

I didn't expect to hear that. I wondered if they just had Spirit Casters lying around in this dimension. I also wondered if that was even a good idea. Last time Kira had a Spirit Caster, she went mad with power. I had to hope that her will was strong enough to handle something with that much power.

We followed him out of the cave system and out onto a path that wrapped itself around the mountain like terrain. There was a balcony that I looked over and from it I saw a sea of sand. It was an endless desert, and we seemed so high above it, as if we were a part of the colorful sky.

"I've never been up so high! This seems higher than any mountain I've ever been on," I gasped.

"That's because we're not *on* a mountain," Aleron told me. "We're on an island."

Kira and I looked back at each other both equally confused.

"I'm sorry but did you just say an island? For it to be an island it would have to be surrounded by water."

He laughed and said, "In your world maybe. But here, our island is surrounded by the sky."

"A floating island? How is that possible?"

"It's possible because our Queen willed it to be that way. Just like the way she wanted the sky to look like that of the deepest parts of the cosmos. And the way she even made this space outside of your own dimension. She is truly a goddess deserving of our worship."

The image of the entire structure was stuck in my mind. A giant golden castle sitting upon the clouds. Just like the engraving of the throne room doors. If King Cole knew about this place then it was clear where he got the imagery from.

To think that their Queen could be so powerful, it definitely blew Kira out of the water. It makes it even more of a relief that Kira was able to work things out to a peaceful conclusion. I wouldn't want to be on the bad side of a vengeful god.

We stopped in front of a cave entrance and went down a set of stairs. The lower we got, the hotter I started to get, and I wasn't a fan of the heat for obvious reasons. Last time I was this hot I couldn't even use my powers.

We finally reached the bottom and were in a large room with lava flowing from the walls and smithing equipment everywhere. Everyone in the room was hard at work, immersing themselves in their own individual projects.

"Abraham!" Aleron shouted. "We have someone here that needs to meet you."

Suddenly a small, bearded man with a muscular physique shot up from behind an anvil and walked over to us while saying, "Crystal, Kira, it's a pleasure to finally meet you two."

He embraced us both at the same time as if we were old friends.

"I'm guessing you were already told we were coming," Kira suggested.

"No, I didn't have to be told. I knew you'd come to me as soon as I sensed that Ice Spirit Caster of yours enter this dimension."

"You sensed my Spirit Caster *specifically*?" I asked.

"Of course. I need to keep track of my creations."

"Your creation? Are you saying that *you* created *my* Spirit Caster."

"Yes, but not just yours. I'm the creator of all Spirit Casters."

"Are you serious?" I asked in complete disbelief.

"Do I look like a liar? Of course I'm serious!" he laughed. "And because of that I can sense where any single Spirit Caster is at any time." He looked over to Kira and said, "I sensed that your Spirit Caster was almost completely destroyed after your father pushed it past its limits. It's a shame really. And I'm guessing it's why you're here now. You want me to make you a new one. Is that right?"

"I don't know," Kira answered while lowering her eyes. "Your Queen told me to come here to get a new one, but I don't know if I'm ready for that. I don't think I'll ever be. That Spirit Caster ruined my life. It took everything I had to shake its control over me. If I get that same weapon again I'm scared of who I'll hurt with it."

Abraham smiled and said, "Kira, you're more than ready for a new Spirit Caster. There was nothing wrong with you or the weapon. The problem was the people who held it before you."

"What exactly do you mean by that?"

"The Dark Spirit Caster was different from most. It's one of my only creations that truly had a mind of its own."

"Wait, are you trying to tell me that my Spirit Caster was alive?"

"Yup. And when your family got ahold of it, it was just in its infancy."

"So it imprinted on them like any child would," I guessed.

"That's correct, Crystal. The Dark Spirit Caster was fueled by a long line of evil hearts, in turn giving a little bit of that evil to its new user. I'll make something entirely new for you Kira. Something that will be a better fit for your purified spirit."

"Thank you," Kira bowed. "You don't know how much this means to me."

"Abraham," I interrupted.

He turned back to me and asked, "What is it?"

"Since you're the creator of these things I feel like this will be my only chance to ask about it. I wanna know how to obtain an Evolved Spirit Caster. I obtained it once before, but I immediately lost the form."

"Ah yes, I saw that in your battle against Kira's father. You achieved the form and sustained it for a moment. That was highly impressive."

"I had so much power. How do I get it back?"

"You can't. Not in your current state at least. Your body is too weak and inexperienced. It can't handle your maximum potential, and let me tell you Crystal, there's a lot of it. You're only at the tip of the iceberg when it comes to your full power. If you were to master all of it you'd become quite the formidable Shēna. You'd probably be even stronger than any Shēna you've ever been in contact with. In fact the only other person in your world that currently has more potential than you is Alizeh Green."

"Wait, you know Alizeh?"

"Of course. She has a Spirit Caster doesn't she? It's a shame how she's stuck in a similar position as you. Her body is so underdeveloped, not because she's weak but because she's so young. If she could reach her full potential then she'd be unstoppable. But we probably won't be seeing that until she's much older."

"If you can sense her Spirit Caster, can you tell me where she is now?"

"She's currently on the move. I believe she's headed towards Nótio Págo."

"Why would she be heading there? She was supposed to be meeting me in Ebony."

"Most likely because Morpheus Morningstar and Arachne Isley are in Nótio Págo too."

"What?" I shouted. "I need to go and help her!"

"That would be pointless. It would take you too long to get there. By the time you reach Nótio Págo, the battle will be long over."

"So you expect me to just let her fight alone?"

"Oh she won't be alone. I can feel another Shēna you know in Nótio Págo who's after the same targets."

It didn't take me too long to figure who that could be. "Rai?" I asked.

He nodded his head and said, "You should let them decide this on their own."

"So I'm just supposed to sit here and do nothing?"

"I would suggest that you sit here and wait for Kira to help you. Once you have her you can use the rest of the forces you have at your disposal to stop them. Better yet, train while you wait. This entire dimension is made up of Rēa. Use that to your advantage and get stronger." He then looked over to Kira and said, "You're Spirit Caster will be ready by tomorrow," before looking her up and down. Her clothes were bloody from being shot before. "You should probably go and get some new clothes while you wait. Aleron, could you show these two where Reshma stays?"

Reshma. That name sounded familiar but I couldn't figure out where I had heard it.

"I didn't think that I'd be turning into a tour guide for a day," Aleron quipped but didn't argue. "Alright, follow me you two."

We followed him out of the cave and back outside seeing a great number of people walk the streets. The city's architecture looked so different from anything I'd ever seen. It was even more advanced than Ebony.

"I'm glad to be changing out of this outfit," Kira claimed. "It's pretty much ruined now. I hope that this *Reshma* person will have something high class."

"Oh, don't worry," Aleron answered. "Reshma is the best seamstress in all of history. That's why our Queen chose for her to be here."

"Best seamstress?" I asked. "I just remembered where I've heard that name from before. It was from another seamstress. She said that Reshma was the best in the world. So much so that she was taken by the gods to be their own personal tailor. I didn't think it was a true story."

"Oh, it's definitely true. It's an honor to wear her brand. It surpasses the class of the rich or even that of Kings and Queens. Gods are meant to wear what she makes."

After walking for a little while longer we finally made it inside to our destination. Threads of silk stuck from the walls and ceiling with a variety of half made clothes hanging from them.

I could see small silkworms hanging on the walls. One of them dropped right on Kira's shoulder, making her jump in fear, swatting it off.

"Disgusting!" Kira said, repulsed by its appearance.

Aleron simply just chuckled and shouted, "Reshma!"

"What is it, my dearly beloved?" We heard a voice coming from the back room. "I'm busy!"

"You have customers."

"Alright, I'm coming."

Reshma came out of the room and into our view. She was a slim and youthful woman with long straight black hair that reached past her lower back. Her skin was dark and her eyes were golden.

She had on a silk rose gold robe with a golden rose insignia on it ironically.

Once Reshma came close she gave Aleron a fairly intimate kiss on the cheek. He didn't react to it and almost ignored it as if he were embarrassed. But he made no attempt to stop her.

"Who are these two?" she asked.

"My name is Kira, and this is Crystal. We were told that—"

"What are you wearing?" Reshma interrupted. "It's torn to shreds." She then looked over to me and said, "And you too. To step foot in this dimension in apparel that drab is an insult for everything I stand for. Take off your clothes. Both of you."

Kira and I looked at each other and then back at her. "You mean, right now?"

"Did I stutter?"

I looked back at Aleron forcing Reshma to say, "What, have you never gotten undressed in front of a man before?"

The thought made me think about the time I spent with Barin and I blushed.

"No it's not that, it's just—"

"Fine!" She interrupted again. "Come with me." She turned and made her way to the back before quickly peeking her head back out and snapped, "Sometime today please!"

Kira and I quickly followed her into the back and took off our clothes so that we wouldn't get yelled at again.

She looked at me and said, "Alright, let's start with you," while pulling out sewing tape. She started measuring my waist while asking, "What's your name?"

"Crystal Winters."

"Well Crystal you have some beautiful hair. White seems to be your color. We'll go with that."

She went over to Kira and looked right at her chest. "Kira was it? What's with this mark? It's unsightly. We'll have to make sure we cover that up."

She was referring to the stab wound I gave her during our battle. It should've been fatal, but she found a way to escape death using *Anástasi,* a transformation that revives the caster and turns them into a monster. I kind of felt bad for giving it to her, but I guess it made us even since she gave me a scar on my hip from our first encounter.

"The red in your eyes is intense. I'll have to incorporate that into yours."

"Can you make it black?" Kira asked. "It's a pretty important color to my bloodline."

"Sure."

Once she was done taking our measurements, she picked our clothes from off the floor, walked over to the fireplace and threw them in.

"You won't be needing these. Here, take these robes and go to the hot springs to clean yourselves. You two are filthy. Come by tomorrow to get your clothes.

CHAPTER TWENTY
KIRA

○

Crystal dipped her foot in the hot spring and said, "I've never felt water this hot before."

I threw off my golden silk robe and walked right in with Crystal soon following behind me. I looked at her exposed pale body. There was a dark mark scarring her hip that I didn't notice before. I couldn't stop staring at it which I noticed made her visibly uncomfortable.

"What is it?" she asked?

"That scar on your hip. What's it from?"

"I got it from you the night we met," she glared. "It was my first ever taste of magic."

"I'm sorry."

"It's whatever now. I gave you that scar on your chest so we're even."

"I'm not just sorry about that. I'm sorry for everything. I've caused you so much pain. Everything that's happened up until this point has been my fault."

She didn't say anything. She didn't even look me in my eyes. She just sat there and stayed silent.

"I want to make everything up to you," I continued. "As soon as I get a new Spirit Caster I'll do everything in my power to help you get your sister back. I know that it doesn't erase everything I've done to you in the slightest, but I hope that you at least won't see me as an enemy and instead as an ally. Or … maybe even a friend."

Her eyes finally met mine with a stone cold look. She still didn't say a word.

"You still hate me don't you? Or I guess a better question is do you still want to kill me? You swore that you would kill me during our battle. I asked before you left Ebony if that was still your goal and you didn't give me an answer. I know that you would have done it if my father didn't intervene so I want to ask again. When this is all over, do you still plan on killing me?"

Her eyes were still cold but somehow became softer. More analyzing. Just like how they looked in our last battle. Before I thought she was trying to analyze how to beat me and that enraged me back then. But in that moment I came to the realization she was just trying to understand who I truly was.

"Kira," she finally spoke, "I—"

"Make sure you soak that wound under the water," someone interrupted.

We both looked back on land and saw a beautiful dark skinned woman with long braids looking right at us.

"I'm sorry but, who are you?" Crystal asked.

"The name's Tallulah," she said with a soothing voice that forced my gaze towards her plump lips. "And yours?"

"Crystal."

"Kira."

"That wound on your shoulder looks pretty bad, Kira. Make sure you keep it under the water."

"Oh it's fine," I told her. "I didn't want any of my blood to get in the water."

"Don't worry about it. This spell is meant to constantly purify whatever it touches. The blood will be cleansed out of the water in a matter of moments."

"Did you just now refer to this hot spring as a spell?"

"Yeah, I did."

"So this water, its heat, and its healing properties are all coming from a Spirit Caster?"

She pulled out her Spirit Caster and said, "Yup, this one right here. The Water Spirit Caster. I call this spell in particular *Thermopigés.*"

"Wait a minute," Crystal interrupted while looking back at me, "doesn't Delta have that same Spirit Caster? Are you telling me that there are Spirit Casters out there that share the same element?"

"Of course," Tallulah answered while raising an eyebrow. "There should be hundreds if not thousands of wands that share the same elements. That should be common knowledge."

"Well it's not as common as it used to be," I told them. "My father, and his father before him have destroyed hundreds of Spirit Casters along with their wielders. They've all become extremely rare. Now the number of Shēna that can be found in a single region along with their Spirit Caster can be counted on a single hand."

"That's disappointing to hear. But expected. The people of earth have always started trouble for themselves."

As she said this, she started taking off her clothes. She removed her shirt revealing the rest of her beautiful skin. Once she was fully undressed I could see her smooth curves. If I didn't already have prior obligations to Ranne, I would have wanted her. Who was I kidding? I wanted her regardless.

She stepped into the water and started to relax, "Can you feel it?"

I definitely was feeling something from her, but I didn't think we were feeling the same thing.

"Feel what?" I asked.

"All the Rēa flowing through you. The water here is rejuvenating. Soaking in here for a day will bring even the elderly back into their prime. It's almost as good as eating a dish made by Sage. His cuisine is the finest I've ever had."

"I've never tried it."

"Well that will have to change. Both of you are coming to dinner with me. Tonight we'll dine with the Queen.

***

A few hours later Crystal and I were sitting at a large round dining room table.

Aleron, the Skoteinós Kósmos Army General. Abraham, the creator of the Spirit Casters. Reshma, the Master Seamstress. Tallulah: the creator of healing water. And of course Céleste, The Cosmic Queen of this dimension. They were all present. There was an extra seat for Ziva, the doctor who helped us before, but she was apparently too busy with work to attend the dinner.

In front of me was a plate filled with foods I'd never seen before. There was a large slab of meat with bones protruding out of it like ribs but the flesh was completely black. Surrounding it was a variety of cut up vegetables... or maybe they were fruits? It didn't look like the most appetizing thing in the world but I thought it would be rude to reject the meal, so I tried it regardless.

I took a single bite and it felt like something poured over my body. The sensation was so soothing and I had felt it before but I couldn't tell when and with what context. The flavor was like an explosion. I got goosebumps from every bite until I finally swallowed.

"Well, what do you think?" Tallulah asked. "Pretty good right?"

"This is the best food I've ever had!" Crystal blurted out with excitement.

"I've had the greatest chefs from all over the Black Continent cook the finest of meals for me throughout my entire life and not once have I ever tasted anything as good as this," I told them. "I'd like to give my compliments to the chef."

"That can easily be arranged," the Queen said before gesturing towards one of her guards. ***"Get Sage in here."***

"At once," he bowed before going into the kitchen. A few moments later he came back out, but this time with a young boy following right behind him. He looked just a little older than Delta; just barley the age of a teenager. His hair was messy and bright red. And his eyes were golden, not too dissimilar from his skin. He kind of reminded me of the flame user that traveled with Crystal.

"Are you the chef?" I asked.

"Yeah," he yawned.

"Well I'm surprised. Your culinary prowess seems to have no bounds."

"Thanks," he said half heartedly. His eyes looked sleepy and his attention was barely on me.

"You'll have to excuse Sage," the Queen told me. **"He puts his Rēa into every meal he makes. I imagine making a large meal like this would drain most of his energy."**

"I'm sorry, did you just say he uses his *Rēa* to cook?"

"I did," she smiled.

"I don't think I follow. I've only ever used it for battle."

Sage cut in by saying "I infuse my Rēa into the food to make it better. It also boosts the amount of Rēa for anyone who consumes it."

His words left me speechless. I couldn't even imagine how a Shēna could do such a thing. But the only conclusion I could come to was that this boy was a lot more skilled with Rēa than anyone *I've* ever met. In fact, everyone at that table seemed to produce that same aura about themselves.

"If that's all then I'll have to ask to be excused. There's still more meals I need to prepare."

"Don't worry yourself Sage," the Queen told him. ***"You've already prepared enough food. Come sit with us and relax."***

"Thank you my Queen," he said with a bow before taking a seat at the table with us.

The Queen turned towards me and said, ***"Tell me, has there been any noteworthy events to occur in your world. It's been a while since I've stepped foot on your planet and I'm curious."***

"Well," I started to say, "there was a recent battle in Ebony that laid waste to more than half the city."

"Who were the invaders?" asked Aleron in a concerned tone.

"Me and a few other friends," answered Crystal.

Everyone at the table seemed surprised by her answer.

"Well you two seemed to have buried the hatchet," Reshma assumed in order to make sense of it. "How long ago did this battle happen?"

Crystal and I looked at each other in our attempt to try and remember the exact date.

"Two weeks ago, probably," I answered.

"It was actually eleven days ago to be precise," Crystal corrected.

Sage took a bite of his own meal and almost immediately gained his vigor back. His eyes looked more lively and his voice much louder.

"Why did you attack Ebony?" he asked Crystal.

"Because Kira killed my parents," Crystal said bluntly. This only made everyone at the table look even more confused. Crystal noticed the awkwardness and quickly tried to correct it by saying, "But it's ok now. I killed her father, so we're even."

Everyone at the table was silent. The only ones at the table who didn't look visibly uncomfortable was Abraham and the Queen. Probably because they already knew this information in one way or another.

"In Kira's defense," Abraham said, "her mind was being manipulated by the Dark Spirit Caster at the time, so I'm partially to blame for some of these events. I've been watching their journey for some time now and I have to tell you, it all makes a lot more sense with context."

"Well luckily I don't care to open up *that* can of worms so let's change the subject," Reshma suggested without any resistance from anyone else at the table, thankfully. "Why are you both here?"

Crystal put down her utensils and seemed to take the conversation a lot more seriously while answering, "Well, recently my sister was kidnapped along with some other people I know. Kira and I have reason to believe that the people who took her were planning on heading here pretty soon."

"Something else that concerns me is the fact that I know the people who are doing this," I added. "They're schemers. Whatever intentions they have with this realm can't be good."

"Do not worry yourself over a matter so trivial, Kira. There is no one in your world that poses a threat to mine.

A mortal being able to even combat me is a laughable thought," the Queen assured me.

"We wouldn't even let it come to that," the General proclaimed. "I would snuff any threat out before it reaches the Queen. Even if they did pose a threat, then I know for a fact that everyone at this table would die before letting our Queen fight."

I admired his resolve and didn't doubt his determination for a second. But the fact that it could even go that far scared me beyond belief.

CHAPTER TWENTY-ONE
ALIZEH

My current goal was to find Morpheus before he sacrificed my father and Crystal's younger sister, Wren. I flew all the way from the edge of Livádia to the center of Nótio Págo and couldn't believe that Crystal could live in such a place. It was freezing, and I couldn't see far past the harsh snow that was raining down. Especially since I only had one good eye left. On top of that, I couldn't remember the last time I had eaten. Perhaps it was before this entire journey.

Either way I was tired. Too tired to continue. I couldn't keep up my flight spell for any longer and went crashing to the ground which was luckily covered by snow.

I didn't feel like getting up. I didn't feel like moving. I had nothing left in me.

The sad thing was that it was so close. I could feel the temple far off in the distance. But it was too far to walk.

Suddenly something caught my attention. Something close. Something familiar. It was someone I knew, but I couldn't tell who.

I trudged through the knee deep snow until I saw a light. A building of some sort. When I got closer I realized it was a tavern.

Whoever I was feeling was in there. I didn't know if they were a friend or a foe but I had to take my chances. Going in there and confronting Morpheus was a better fate than staying out and freezing anyways.

I opened up the door and saw that the tavern was crowded. I zoned in on the Rēa I was sensing and looked past the sea of faces to see one that was more special than the rest.

Their beautiful dark skin like midnight personified. Their curls were almost as white as the snow on their boots. And their golden eyes looked into mine with the same shock that I had felt from spotting them.

They jumped up and ran over to me pushing through the crowd.

"Alizeh?" they called getting close enough to hug me.

"Rai?" I called back. But I couldn't get an answer back because before they could even give me one I could feel myself falling and passing out from exhaustion.

***

I woke up with a young boy I had never seen before standing over me with outstretched arms. His hair was blond and his eyes were green like mine. I laid in bed while he was performing some kind of spell on me with a Spirit Caster. Whatever his intentions were, they couldn't be trusted.

As soon as I got my bearings, I grabbed his arm with one hand and my Spirit Caster with the other.

"Who are you?" I shouted, ready to strike.

"Aeson!" he yelped back, throwing his arm in the air. "My name is Aeson!"

"Paírno Ptísi," I said, causing my body to fly up and onto my feet. I grabbed him by the collar and hoisted him up into the air. "Where am I? What were you doing to me?" I shouted.

At that moment the door opened and Rai walked through it with a loaf of bread and a pitcher of water.

They tilted their head in confusion over our situation and asked, "Am I interrupting something? I can come back later if you—"

Before they could finish I dropped the boy to the ground and hurled myself at Rai to hold them tight. I couldn't believe it. Seeing them gave me so much relief to the point where I started crying almost instantly after touching them.

"Alizeh, are you crying?" Rai asked in an almost annoyed tone. "I just saw you last week."

"I know, I know. It's just ... I've had a really rough couple of days," I told them as I wiped away my tears.

"Tell me about it."

And I did. They told me about their meeting with Crystal, letting me know that they already knew about my situation. I told them about my adventures in the desert and my findings from it, causing them to tell me about how they found Aeson and how they knew to come here. I spoke with them while sitting on the bed with a blanket draped over me. Even more importantly, I was able to eat a loaf of bread and drink a hot cup of cocoa.

"It sounds like you really *did* have it rough," Rai finally admitted.

Having them acknowledge it didn't make me feel any better about my situation.

"Alizeh," Rai continued. "We'll save your father, along with my grandmother, and Aeson's brother."

"I hope so. I just don't know if I'll be a big help. Ever since my last battle, my vision isn't what it used to be. I can't see out of my right eye at all."

"Aeson might be able to fix that."

I looked over at the boy and asked, "Really? How?"

The quiet boy spoke softly, "My Spirit Caster allows me to heal wounds and illnesses, but I've never had to heal a wound that severe before. I don't know if I can do it."

"Can you try?"

He nodded his head, walked over to me and placed his hand over my scarred eye.

"*Therapévo,*" he spoke.

The darkness that clouded my vision started to clear up. Soon I saw light, which eventually turned into color, and before I knew it my eye was back to normal. It was a miracle yet he looked disappointed when he took his hand away from my face.

"I'm sorry," he told me, "I couldn't heal your scar."

I immediately hugged him and said, "Thank you Aeson! I can see thanks to you so who cares about a stupid scar?" I let go of him and went to the single mirror in the room to see how bad it looked. "And besides, it kind of makes me look pretty cool don't you think? I'm like a *little* Ana."

Rai laughed and said, "Yup, you're as cool as they come."

I turned to them and asked, "When are we leaving?"

"As soon as this storm clears up. But that probably won't happen until morning. So for now we need to get as much rest as possible. We'll need to be at our best tomorrow if we plan on getting our families back."

CHAPTER TWENTY-TWO
ANA

I walked into the room where my mother was staying to see her still in bed and fast asleep. Blood covered her blankets from a wound I couldn't see. Immediately realizing that it wasn't the right time for me to talk to her, I turned around to exit until her words stopped me.

"Ana," she called. "Where are you going?"

I turned back to see her sitting up. I could now see the scar I left on her face and her arm covered in bloody bandages. Her right hand was gone because of my actions.

The sight broke me, and I couldn't control my body from running to grab her. I couldn't control the emotions that forced me to cry out to her.

"I'm sorry mom!" I screamed. "I'm so sorry."

She raised her only hand slowly to my face, wiping away my tears while lifting it up to meet her soft gaze.

"I haven't seen you cry since your father passed. For such a long time you've devoted yourself to strength. And now that you've finally achieved it you're starting to realize it's a little more than you've bargained for."

"Am I unworthy of this power?" I clenched.

"No. You've earned it. You told me that you saw your father when you achieved it. You've gained his favor along with my own. Now you must learn another skill to accompany it. Restraint."

Restraint. I knew the meaning but still somehow that word sounded foreign to me. I threw away restraint to gain power. Every battle I've ever had I jumped into without hesitation and have shown my opponent no mercy unless they themselves have shown such kindness.

And as if she heard my thoughts of defiance, she continued, "Not everything needs to be a battle."

"Well," I chuckled while wiping away my tears, "That's not going to be a big problem for me anymore."

"Why's that?" she raised her brow.

"Because, my Warriors Spirit ... it's gone."

"What do you mean *gone*?"

"I can't activate it anymore. After what I did to you ... I can't feel any of that power left."

"You make it sound like it's the end," she scoffed.

"Everything I've worked towards is gone!" I snapped back. "And didn't you *just* say I should stop fighting."

She rolled her eyes and shook her head, "Still so hardheaded. I didn't say to stop fighting. You simply need to choose your battles. You're unbalanced."

"And how exactly do I find that balance?"

"It's not something you can simply just find. You have to create it. Don't be reckless in your pursuit of power. And don't show cowardice in the face of adversity. Stay courageous for the benefit of your own virtues."

She laid back while giving an exaggerated sigh. "Coming up with all this wise guidance is making me tired."

I stood back up while wiping away my tears, "Alright, get some rest. I've got some things I need to do anyway.

I turned around and walked out of the room, where Cara was leaning against the wall outside the door waiting for me.

"You ready?" she asked.

"Yeah," I told her. "Let's have one more battle to break past our limits."

This will be her second battle to the death. And this time we weren't stopping until we saw results.

CHAPTER TWENTY-THREE
ARACHNE

Morpheus, Thelonious, and I walked across the frozen bridge with a large floating amalgamation of rocks smashed together to make a rough sphere following right behind us. It was the prison we used to keep our captives trapped. Having Thelonious with us definitely made it easier hauling them around. He was useful. Although I have to say I wasn't a fan of having an extra person intruding in on our plans. Luckily Morpheus told me that he was only a temporary addition. Just another pawn in his game.

We walked past two guards who didn't even flinch at our presence. That was all thanks to Morpheus's illusions. We were invisible. His ability made this a cakewalk.

Once we made it into the temple, we saw two women sparring each other. They were skilled and their battle seemed fierce as they fought with deadly weapons. It would have been trouble if we had to face them. As we walked past, one of them stopped and stared right at me. The three of us stopped in place. She looked familiar but I couldn't place where I had seen her before. She had dark skin, long locks and an eyepatch covering her right eye.

I leaned in close to Morpheus and whispered, "Are you sure your spell is working right?"

Morpheus glared back at her.

The woman who didn't seem to notice us said, "What's wrong Ana? You seem distracted."

"Do you see anything strange over there?" asked Ana.

"What do you mean?"

"The light. Something's off about it. And I could have sworn I heard someone else in here."

"It's probably just your imagination."

"Maybe…"

Ana quickly kicked up her spear from off the floor, caught it, and chucked it right past Morpheus's face. The light around us started to flicker and disperse. The spell was undone!

"She saw through it!" Morpheus shouted.

"Morpheus?" Ana called in shock. "Cara, we have intruders!" she continued. "Alert everyone!"

Her friend ran out of the room but Ana stayed to face us. She ran towards us without hesitation.

Morpheus scoffed and ordered, "Thelonious, take her out."

Thelonious pulled out his Spirit Caster, pointed it at her and said, ***"Pétagma Rok."*** A chunk of earth was ripped up from the floor and flung itself right at her, but she narrowly evaded it and continued her pursuit. Before she got close enough to grab us,

Thelonious let out the spell, ***"Pétrinos Toíchos."*** A rock wall formed right in between her and us forcing her to run right into it. He then swiped his wand and the wall flew off the ground pushing her along with it. Before it slammed into the wall, she pushed herself off of it, rolling onto the floor.

Her reaction time was amazing. I'd never seen anything like it. And the way she moved reminded me of Ranne at her best. It didn't even look like she busted a sweat yet. I then remembered exactly who this woman was. She was one of Crystal's allies. The Zubarian of the group.

She sprinted towards us once again from the other side of the room causing Thelonious to say, "You're a persistent one aren't you?"

"It's my job!" Ana shouted with the unwavering goal to take us down.

"You're only human. Just give up!"

"I'm more than human!"

Suddenly more people ran into the room like a stampede ready to swarm us.

"Looks like we'll have to get our hands dirty," Morpheus said while pulling out his dagger. I took out my Spirit Caster with the intent to kill.

"Ékrixi Tis Gis!"

The ground beneath them shook and exploded upwards like a landslide taking down a good chunk of them. Morpheus created a multitude of clones that acted as after images. With them he ran through the crowd slicing up every one in his path using his dagger. And I used *Bála Oxéos* to shoot balls of acid at whoever I saw, burning them until they were an unrecognizable corpse. In less than a minute we had taken almost all of them down.

Morpheus pressed an attack on Ana, swinging his daggers at her and hitting almost every time thanks to his illusions. But someone came and interrupted the battle. It was the same girl from before. The one named Cara. She threw a golden sword towards them and Ana caught it before swinging it in every direction, forcing Morpheus to back off.

"I should've known you weren't going to make this easy for us," Morpheus groaned.

Ana pointed her blade towards him and asked, "Make *what* easy for you? Why are you even here? Did Kira send you? To think I actually believed scum like her could change."

Suddenly Morpheus disappeared out of sight and appeared right in front of her, already sticking his dagger deep into her chest.

"You actually think that I'd take orders from a spoiled brat like Kira? Who the hell do you take me for?"

Morpheus went in for another strike but was stopped by a spear that flew right past his face. It came from Cara and she was running right towards them. Once again Morpheus disappeared out of sight and soon reappeared by Thelonious and I.

Cara ran to Ana and asked, "Are you ok?"

"Don't worry about me!" Ana ordered. "Keep your eyes on the enemy."

Before it could be carried out Morpheus looked to Thelonious and said, "Crush them."

And with a flick of his wrist, Thelonious made a part of the ceiling collapse in on them. They were buried and even if they survived, they were no longer a threat to us.

"Well that was easy," I laughed.

"Let's keep moving," Morpheus ordered. "We need to find those runestones."

We started to make our way out of the room, but someone stood in the way of the exit.

"I'm sorry but I can't allow you to do that," she said. She was old and had an eye patch over one eye. She was also missing a hand and was armed with nothing but a knife.

Morpheus looked at her with an unfazed look and asked, "Are you the elder of this temple?"

"That I am," she answered.

"Then you must know where the rune stones are."

"You three aren't allowed here. Leave at once or there will be consequences."

Morpheus laughed and said, "I don't think you're in the position to be making threats. We've taken on your army and they weren't even worth our attention." He walked towards her and continued saying, "If you don't tell me what I want to know then I'll kill you."

"I'd die before telling the likes of *you* anything."

"Then who am I to deny that request?"

He reached his hand out towards her but she quickly pushed it away and thrusted her fist into his sternum. The knife in her hand started to glow and then there was an explosion of light that blinded me for a moment. When my eyes adjusted I saw that Morpheus was gone and in his wake was a crater that stretched all the way past us and led to a massive hole in the wall. It seemed that he was blasted out of the temple and was nowhere in sight.

"M-Morpheus!" I cried.

"What the hell was that?" Thelonious shouted. "Is she a Shēna?"

"Don't compare me to your kind," she said with a piercing red eye, "My name is Aza and I come from the Zubarian clan. Our weapons are stronger than that of a Spirit Caster. Now this is your last warning. Leave before I—"

Her boast was short-lived. Morpheus appeared right behind her and stabbed her in the back forcing her to fall to the ground.

"Ahh I see," he spoke. "I can see why the Royal family wanted to wipe you out before they went after the Shēna. You people truly are dangerous."

Aza fell right to the ground one step away from death. I shouldn't have worried about Morpheus. He's too cunning to fall for such a trick. He truly was already a god amongst men.

"Arachne, Thelonious. Let's go."

We left her body and explored the temple until we found a set of stairs.

"I can feel it down here," he said before leading us down and into a hall. There was a door that we could feel a large amount of Rēa coming from.

Morpheus placed his hand on the door and said, "This is it. Thelonious, let them out."

Thelonious looked back at the large chunk of earth and it started crumbling away. A green mist started to pour out along with our captives. The mist was a part of my spell, *Aério Ypnou* which was a sleeping gas. They had been knocked out within that rock this whole time.

"Arachne, wake up the girl," Morpheus ordered.

I walked up to her, pulled out my wand and placed the tip next to her upper lip.

"Ammonía," I said.

Wren woke up instantly gasping for air as if she had just been revived from the dead. She had a look of terror on her face and tried to crawl away but we had her surrounded.

"Get up kid," I told her. "It's time to make yourself useful."

"Where am I? Who are you? What do you want?" She started to cry.

"What are you deaf, kid? I said get up!"

"Arachne, don't be so harsh with your words," Morpheus told me. "She's just a child after all." He crouched down to meet with her and said, "To answer your questions, you are back in your home country, Nótio Págo. My name is Morpheus and I desperately need your help."

"I want to go home," Wren cried. "I want my sister!"

"Oh don't cry, Wren," he told her while gently wiping away her tears. "I promise to let you go as long as you just do two things for me."

"Just two things?"

"Yup," he smiled.

"You promise?"

"I'm a man of my word."

"What do you want me to do?"

"I need you to open this door. It was made to react to your bloodline."

"How do I open it?"

"All you have to do is touch it."

Wren got up and slowly inched her way towards the door.

"Hurry up. We don't have all day," I groaned.

She finally placed her palm on the door, and it started to glow with the pattern of bright snowflakes. Once she took her hand off, the door started to open on its own with chilling mist spewing out.

Morpheus picked up Tal while Thelonious picked up Tora and we all walked into the room. There were rune symbols carved all over the stone walls. Morpheus put down Tal and walked over to a small stone pillar in the center of the room. He unraveled a pouch from his side and poured its contents on the pedestal. It was the shattered pieces of the Dark Spirit Caster.

Then he reached into his pocket and pulled out feathers. But these weren't just any feathers. They came straight from that flaming monstrosity of Phoenix Island.

He looked back at Wren and said, "Ok, now I just need one more thing. Just stand still for me. Can you do that?"

She nodded her head and he said, "Good." He looked up at the ruins and started reciting the words.

"Phoenix feathers burn
Let the darkness surge through me
Ascend my body
Sýntixi."

Suddenly three beams of energy shot out from Morpheus, the wand, and the feathers and stretched towards our three captives instantly piercing into their souls. Tora and Tal instantly woke up with cries of pain but they were drowned out by the screams of Wren.

She was just a kid. This was probably the first time she had ever felt such pain. Her screams were so horrific to the point where even I had to look away.

Then something got my attention. It got *everyone's* attention. And it came in the form of Rēa.

"Do you two feel that?" Morpheus asked.

"Yeah," I answered. "There are two or more high level Shēna coming right for us."

"Handle them and don't let them reach me. If you fail, everything we've worked so hard for up till this point will be for nothing."

CHAPTER TWENTY-FOUR
ALIZEH

As soon as the sun came up Aeson, Rai and I left the tavern and made our way to the Temple.

"Are you sure this is the right direction?" Rai shouted as we ran side by side with Aeson on their back.

"Yeah, I'm sure. There's a lot of Rēa coming from that way. But there's definitely something off about it."

"What do you mean?"

"I don't know how to explain it. Let's just focus on getting there as quickly as possible."

"Alright," he nodded.

After putting all our energy into running with our spells, it didn't take too long for us to get to the temple.

"So this is the place huh?" Rai said, "I can finally feel it. All the Rēa flowing from here. The air is thick."

"They're here. I can feel them. Let's go."

"Aeson," Rai called, "you ready for this?"

"I think so," Aeson gulped.

The three of us walked into the temple and saw dozens of bodies scattered around the place. Some I could feel were still alive while I didn't need my sixth sense to know that most had died. There was blood everywhere and their bodies were badly burned with some even missing limbs as if they'd been melted off the bone.

I'd never seen such a horrific scene and I doubt that the others had a different experience. Aeson ran to the corner and started vomiting on the floor while Rai tried to avoid looking at the more grotesque parts of the room.

"Who's there?" I heard someone say from across the room. I looked over and saw that it was an old woman laying in a puddle of her own blood. Rai and I quickly made it over to her.

"Are you ok?" Rai asked. "What happened here?"

"Her life force is fading fast," I told Rai. "I don't think she's going to make it."

"I probably won't," she accepted. "Are you Shēna?"

"Yes, we are," Rai answered.

"That's good ... We were attacked by three other Shēna and you few are the last line of defense. They're still here and plan on using our ruins to gain an unimaginable amount of power. I'm sorry to put this on you children, but you need to stop them before they can achieve their goal."

"Don't worry," I grabbed her hand. "We'll stop them."

"Thank you."

Rai looked to Aeson and asked, "Can you save her?"

"It will take a while, but it should be possible."

"Then get to it. Alizeh and I are gonna find the people who did this."

Aeson got to work on the old lady, and Rai got up to make their way out of the room. I picked myself up to follow but I found myself sitting right back down after the floor shook. It was like an earthquake and the floor around us started to collapse.

Rai looked back at us and yelled, "Get back!" Right after their warning, the floor fell around them and they were gone. The floor around Aeson and I started to collapse as well, but I was *not* going to be a victim to another cave-in like so many times before.

I grabbed Aeson by the collar while using my speed spell to jump away from the uneven ground. Unfortunately I wasn't fast enough to grab the old woman and she too, just like Rai, fell with half of the temple. When all the dust finally settled, the side of the temple that Aeson and I were on was still standing. But the other side fell victim to a landslide. It practically slid halfway down the small mountain.

I went to the edge and shouted, "Rai!"

But there was no answer from anyone down there. This entire situation seemed off. This didn't feel like a natural disaster, but forced. Probably by someone's magic. But I didn't know who could've possibly possessed so much power.

Aeson looked the other way and gulped before answering the question in my head.

"Thelonious."

I turned around to see a lean young man with scruffy brown hair and eyes. It was the same man that I had fought when this all started. The earth user who helped Arachne take my father and poison my mother. And somehow Aeson knew him too.

"Why are you here, Aeson?" Thelonious asked. "Did you change your mind on Morpheuses' proposal?"

"I came here for you!" Aeson shouted back trying his best to not falter.

"So, you came to fight?"

"No! I came here to bring you back home."

"Seriously? You know I can't do that. Morpheus offered us great power, more than we can even comprehend. I've come too far to just give up on the promise."

"Well I've come too far to give up on you."

"Well you should. I've been given the orders to kill anyone who gets in the way of Morpheuses' plan. Don't think for one second that just because we have the same mother means I'll spare you."

"Brother, I told you I don't want to fight!"

I finally stepped in front of Aeson and cut in not wanting to waste any more time on the family related squabble.

"Don't worry Aeson," I told him while walking towards Thelonious. "You don't have to fight him. Just stand back and support me from afar while I handle him."

"And who are you supposed to be? His *backup*?" Thelonious teased. "Oh wait, I remember you. You're that girl that I almost killed a few nights ago. You really think you can beat me, kid?"

"No, I actually think I can *kill* you," I threatened. "But since your Aeson's brother I'm only gonna hurt you real bad for wasting my time."

I released my Rēa causing Aeson to jump in fear behind me but his older brother stood tall and on guard. He wasn't scared of me. That would be his undoing.

I lunged myself at him, but before I could reach him, he put up a wall of earth blocking my path. He had an Evolved Earth Spirit Caster. And the power emanating from it felt so familiar. Could that be the same wand that Adam held? In the end it didn't matter. I'd still beat him just like I did with Adam.

I quickly circled around the wall and made my way behind. Once he spotted me, he put up another wall but that was just a feint attack. I jumped over the wall making my way above him and shouted, "***Enischyméni Michanikí Diátrisi!***" I threw a punch down at him and the force of it slammed him into the ground while forcing a cloud of dust into the air.

Before the dust cleared, I landed back on the ground and told him, "This isn't my first time fighting against someone who held that wand. I know all its tricks and I can see you're a complete novice. Why don't you just make this easy on yourself and give up?"

There was no answer. For a moment I thought he had already been knocked out, but I didn't take him for *that* much of a weakling. I swiped my Spirit Caster through the air forcing all the dust to blow away, but to my surprise he was nowhere to be seen.

The next thing I knew I felt something grab my ankles and pull my body underground, leaving only my head exposed. Before I could even realize what happened, Thelonious quickly dug himself from underground like a weasel and kicked me right in my head with all his strength. He kicked me so hard that I think a couple of teeth shattered in my mouth.

I underestimated him. This was a new spell I had never seen before. He used the smoke as a cover to dig himself into the ground using his magic. I was careless and was paying for it dearly.

"Alizeh!" Aeson shouted while pointing his Spirit Caster at me from afar. Once he did this the pain went away almost instantly. He healed me but unfortunately that didn't stop Thelonious from attacking again.

He kicked me again with the same amount of force, but this time I could feel my nose cave in as blood splattered all around me. I had never experienced such pain in my life.

"Stop it, Thelonious!" Aeson shouted while healing me again and once again taking away the pain.

"I can do this all day, Aeson," Thelonious taunted. "I know you, however, have a limit to how much you can heal someone. Let's test it!"

Thelonious rose his hand up making large rocks from the rubble around us float and threw them all in my direction. Before they could hit, Aeson shouted, "***Moudiasménos!***"

Once the rocks hit, I expect a hard impact, which of course there was but I didn't feel it. Blood still spewed from my mouth and nose but this time there was no pain to accompany it. This must've been a part of his spell. Aeson continued to heal me after the fact, but Thelonious was right. Aeson couldn't keep this up forever.

"Aeson!" I shouted. "You have to fight! We can't beat him like this!

"I can't!" Aeson cried. "He's my brother."

Thelonious placed his boot on my face like a stepping stool and told me, "You put too much faith in my brother. He's a coward who never deserved that wand!" Thelonious swiped his wand at Aeson forcing the rocks to pelt him until he finally flew back and hit the ground. "That wand was *my* birthright, and he stole it from me! Our mother chose him for what? Because he was *kinder* than me? It's the most asinine thing I've ever heard of in my life!" Thelonious then waved his Spirit Caster and lifted a giant boulder over my head while walking away to not get himself crushed with me. "Kindness and compassion are a weakness. It doesn't equal strength and I know that now."

Aeson slowly picked himself up while saying, "You're wrong Thelonious. Kindness is more powerful than you think. Just like how the sun can melt ice, kindness and mercy have the potential to melt sadness, hostility and distrust."

Thelonious, merely scoffed at the statement and released his spell to drop the boulder on my head, but this time the attack didn't hit.

"***Steroeidés!***" Aeson shouted and within a blink of an eye, he lunged towards us and smashed the boulder into pieces with his bear fist.

"What?" Thelonious gasped.

I was equally just as shocked. For a split second, he was almost as fast as me, if not *faster*. And that strength ... I didn't understand how he could have hid that from me. It seems like once again I had underestimated someone in battle. But this time it was a welcomed mistake.

"How did you do that?" Thelonious asked, too stunned to move.

"I'd explain it to you but the thing is, I can only use this spell for a limited amount of time. I know that my words won't reach you, so I'll have to use this spell to drag you back home by force."

Aeson wasted no time charging towards his brother. Thelonious put up a rock wall to stop him, but it didn't even slow him down. He rammed himself right through like a bull and punched his brother right in the face, sending him flying across the room.

"Aeson, you're so cool!" I cheered him on but that only stopped him, causing him to blush.

"Th-thank you."

"Also, I know you're busy, but can you please get me out of here as soon as humanly possible?"

"Oh yeah, sorry."

He quickly ran over, grabbed me by the collar and picked me from the ground like a vegetable.

"Thanks," I smiled.

"No!" we heard Thelonious shout, bloodied and beaten from just a single punch. "No, no, no, no, no!"

"I think you broke him," I teased to Aeson but he looked back at Thelonious with a serious look.

"I'm not going to be beaten by children!" Thelonious finally said something tangible in his tantrum. "Especially not by a weak little shit like you, Aeson!" He slammed his Spirit Caster into the ground and shouted, "***Stratós Vromiás!***"

The earth started to glow beneath our feet and every stray rock and small piece of rubble started to stack into multiple pillars around us. Soon they started to take the form of people and before we knew it, we were surrounded by an army of rock monsters. This fight was far from over and everyone knew that.

Aeson put his back to mine and asked, "How are we going to handle something like *this*? We're completely surrounded!"

"Isn't it obvious?" I smirked. "We fight!"

CHAPTER TWENTY-FIVE
RAI

I woke up, freezing and covered in rubble. It didn't take much to dig myself out and see that I was outside at the ridge of the mountain that the temple sat on. I couldn't really remember what had happened until I heard the coughing.

I turned and saw the woman laying not too far behind me, still clinging to life. I quickly crawled to her to see if she was ok, but it still didn't look like she was going to make it, and I had no idea where Aeson was to heal her. I wasn't even sure if *he* or Alizeh for that matter were still alive.

"Aeson! Alizeh! Are you guys out there? I need help now!" I called out while looking in every direction.

The woman grabbed me by the arm to get my attention and said, "There's no time. You need to go now."

"I can't just leave you here. We can save you."

"You're very kind, young one," she grinned as drops of blood stained her lips. "What's your name?"

"Rai," I answered.

"Ahh now I see. You're one of Ana's new friends. I'm happy that she'll have such helpful people by her side when I'm gone."

"Wait, you know Ana? How? Who are you?"

She didn't answer a single question. The light left her eyes before she could. I didn't know who this woman was but for some reason it felt like I had lost someone close to me. Closer than I could even comprehend. Especially since she was a friend of Ana's.

Right in that same moment I heard the sound of something cracking. I looked up and saw a cave opening up from the mountain as if it were a monster widening its jaws. Someone walked out of the cave. A Shēna I presumed before getting a good look at their face. Who else would be able to summon such power?

"Rai!" she called. "It's been a while."

It was Arachne. One of the people we've been looking for. And I knew exactly how dangerous she was. If I let her stall for too long then she'd poison me before the battle could even start. I wasn't going to let her get that far.

"***Vima Flas***," I whispered under my breath. With it, my speed was boosted and I used that speed to dart away from the woman and right towards Arachne before she could get another word in. When I got close enough I yelled, "***Alexikéravno!***", causing a small blade of electricity to surround my Spirit Caster as I attacked.

I aimed right at her chest, but she narrowly dodged the attack, pulled out her dagger and sliced my arm before I could retreat. It was just a scratch, so I dismissed it and pressed on with the attack.

Arachne jumped back to get some distance, but I wasn't going to let her get away.

I pointed my Spirit Caster in her direction and shouted, *"Astrapiaía Lónchi!"*

The blade of lightning stretched out like a spear and pierced her right through her chest. Once I dismissed the spell, she fell right down to the ground with a hole in her chest while coughing up heaps of blood. I didn't think it would be that easy.

Arachne was as good as dead and unlike a certain ally of hers, I didn't see any point in trying to save her. Especially after what she did to Alizeh's family. She deserved to die. And so did Morpheus. I turned my back on her and made my way to the cave. That's most likely where he was.

"Wait," Arachne choked. "You can't just … leave me here to die."

I ignored her and kept walking.

"If you do leave me here," she continued, "then you'll never find out… what I did with your grandmother."

That got my attention. I stopped and turned around with the intent to kill her if I didn't like her answer.

"What did you do to her?" I asked.

Arachne didn't answer me. She just let out a weak laugh. I walked back over to her and picked her up by the collar, raising her high above me.

"Answer me!" I roared with electricity shooting from my body. Blood from her wound splattered all over my body, all the way from my face to my chest.

"What you need to know about your grandmother," she finally answered with a grin, "Is that she's as good as dead."

She then grabbed my arm where she first cut me and whispered the spell, "*Die.*"

Before I knew it, with just a single second, the part of my arm that she was touching had completely disintegrated and I could do nothing but watch as half of my right arm fell to the snow. I dropped Arachne along with it and sat there screaming in pain and shock from the loss of my arm.

Arachne laughed over my screams and continued, "Did you really think it would be that easy to kill me without coming out unscathed? You should have been more careful. I injected that poison in you as soon as I cut you. And you wanna know something funny? That blood that's covering your body isn't normal blood."

Once she said that I looked down at myself and realized I was covered in her blood. And right then I felt it burn. I could feel my skin melt, forcing me to fall into the snow to try and cool it down. But it didn't work. It just got hotter and hotter. I screamed and cried as I saw no end to the suffering.

"Yeah ... That's going to hurt like hell," she continued, "but unfortunately, it's not going to kill you. Might leave a few nasty scars though. And it'll slow you down making it harder for you to stop Morpheus. I'm just sad that I won't be alive to see what becomes of this world when he's done with it."

CHAPTER TWENTY-SIX
ALIZEH

Piles of rocks and dust laid at our feet yet they still just kept coming. This army of dirt felt never ending and we were incredibly outgunned. I still had a little fight in me, but I couldn't say the same about Aeson.

When I realized he was panting heavily next to me I asked, "What's wrong? Are you tired?"

"I don't know how much longer I can do this for," he answered. He had sweat all over his face and his knuckles were bloody from constantly punching these rock monsters. And he sniffled as if he were going to cry. Before, he said that his strength boosting spell could only last so long. He was probably at his limit. This was probably his first fight and it was a tough one. He had a long way to go before he could reach the rest of us when it came to stamina.

And there was also another factor. He was fighting his brother. Possibly to the death. This battle was obviously taking a mental toll on him.

"Well I can do this all day," I told him. "Take a break and give me some support from afar just like before."

"You know, that's actually a good idea," he said as I could feel him powering down. He then tapped his wand against my arm and said, "*Steroeidés.*"

Right then and there I felt my Rēa skyrocket, and I felt *way* stronger than before. Way stronger than I'd ever felt. "Woah! What the heck did you just do to me?"

"I'm boosting your power but only for a few minutes. Any longer and it can be fatal so end this quickly."

"Got it," I grinned before using a spell releasing my full power. Wind blew in every direction blowing everything away. I held onto Aeson while every single rock monster was destroyed under the weight of my hurricane. The temple wasn't strong enough to handle my power and was torn apart and completely destroyed. I didn't mean to let out this much power. I looked down at my Spirit Caster and once again saw that it had evolved. But this time it felt more stable. And my anger wasn't the trigger. This must've been the effect of Aeson's spell and one that I'd probably need again in the future.

I looked around and saw multiple bodies fly high into the air. They were innocent bystanders from the earlier fight. I needed to calm myself even more, so as to not hurt them.

I slowed down my winds to make everyone descend back to the ground as slowly as possible. But then something, or I guess someone caught my eye. A beautiful dark-skinned woman with long locks and an eye patch was one of the people currently in my grasp. It couldn't have been ... Ana? What was she doing here?

Was she dead? Did those monsters *kill* her? No. She was covered in blood but I could still feel her. It was faint, but she was alive. This must've been her home. The ice temple she once told me about. Now in ruin.

They hurt her and her family in their own home. One of my closest friends. I wasn't going to let them get away with this! This fight just became personal.

I put her and every other bystander back on the ground before completely stopping the winds and looked around to see where Thelonious was. I caught a glimpse of Aeson staring up at the sky and I turned my head in the same direction. Thelonious was standing atop a floating rock high in the air.

"We should go up there and finish this," I told Aeson. He nodded his head but before we could actually do anything about it, once again the earth started shaking beneath our feet. I could see in the distance giant chunks of the earth were being uprooted and flew into the sky. The entire landscape as far as my eye could see was being completely ravaged. But this wasn't the part that was supposed to hurt us. Soon every rock, boulder, and chunk of a mountain that floated into the sky started to join with each other, creating an even larger chunk of earth in the air. For a moment it looked like there was a second moon above us. Then it started to fall.

"Alizeh, that thing's bigger than a mountain and it's heading right for us!" Aeson gasped.

"If that thing lands then it won't just kill us!" I explained. "It has the potential to destroy all of Nótio Págo if not the whole Black Continent and I don't know if I have the power to stop it!"

"Then I'll give you *my* power. Every last drop."

"That'll have to be enough. Hold on to me from behind."

"Why?"

"Aeson, just do it!"

He quickly scurried over and wrapped his arms around my sh oulder."Now what?" he asked.

"Hold on tight. We're bringing the fight to him. ***Paírno Ptísi!***"

We then shot up into the air heading straight towards the giant asteroid.

"I'm going to attack that thing with everything I've got," I told him. "I need you to give me the energy to make that possible. I'll probably be out of the fight either way after this, so it'll be up to you to finish off your brother. Do you think you'll be able to do that?"

"I know I will."

"That's what I like to hear!"

I started to raise my power as we flew closer to the massive rock and used the spell, "***Gale Lance!***" It created a large spiral of wind around my Evolved Spirit Caster. That within itself was not going to put a scratch on this rock. At least not until I felt all of Aeson's Rēa flow into me. All of his strength. All of his power. Every ounce of his heart. It made my attack overwhelming even for me. The spiral of wind spread even larger and covered our entire bodies. It grew bigger and bigger until it turned us into the tip of a giant tornado.

Once we made contact with the rock, we drilled into it causing sparks and a burst of color to explode around us. It must've been from the sheer amount of Rēa clashing against each other. Our power together was literally bending the fabric of space around us.

It hurt drilling through the rock. It felt like my bones were breaking, as if my body itself was the drill wearing down. Once we made it to the center, I stopped the attack and used a new one hoping that we were deep enough to destroy this thing from the inside out.

"Enischyméni Michanikí Diátrisi!"

I balled my fist up and punched the very center of the asteroid. There was a flash of light and fire that blew everything back with its burst of colors including Aeson and I. I couldn't feel or see anything past the lights and smoke. I knew I was falling but it didn't matter. The destruction around me was beautiful and somewhat soothing. But that was just because I felt empty. I used up all my energy. I couldn't continue. I had to leave this up to Aeson and for the first time in a while I could finally rest.

CHAPTER TWENTY-SEVEN
RAI

I must've passed out from the pain, because when I opened my eyes I saw a meteor shower rain down from the sky. Chunks of flaming rocks fell down all around me. It had to be from a fight. Alizeh was still fighting. I had to get up and do something.

I tried to move my arm to pick myself up, but I couldn't feel it. It was really gone. And even though blood was pouring from where it used to be, it was still the least of my problems. I still had to find my grandmother.

I finally was able to pick my mangled body up from off the ground and turn my sights to the cave that Arachne originally came out of. Morpheus had to be in there. I had to end this.

I stumbled into the cave while holding the wall. It was hard to stand. Even harder to walk. But I pressed on until I saw a blue light at the end of the tunnel.

Once I reached the end I was in a small cavern. I saw my grand-mother floating in the air with two other people I had never seen before. A man and a young girl. They all screamed in pain as the Rēa was being torn out of their bodies and being brought right to the center of the cavern. That's where Morpheus was standing. He was taking their very life essence.

"Grandma!" I cried.

Morpheus looked back at me and said, "You're too late." And with that the ritual ended. They all fell to the ground with little to no life in their bodies.

I used all my strength to run past Morpheus and to my grandmother but fell right on my face just shy of reaching her. I had to drag myself the rest of the way.

"Grandma, are you ok?"

"I feel weak," she answered. "It might be my time."

"No!" I cried. "I have lightning! Electricity, remember? It gives life. I can save you."

"No, it won't work. You'll just end up killing yourself trying to save me."

"You don't know that!"

"I do know," she huffed. "Remember, I'm the one who taught you how to use that thing."

I pressed my face into her chest to stop myself from screaming. She was right. I didn't have any energy left in me. It probably wouldn't be enough and my own life force would be used up in the process. She truly was going to die and there was nothing I could do about it.

"I heard you beat the king," she said, grabbing my attention to look back up at her. "I'm so proud of you. And you had great allies to help you along the way. I know things look bad right now but don't lose hope. You embody lightning... the most powerful force in nature. You can destroy and shine brilliantly while doing it. With help you can beat him too. Remember who you are. You're Rai Leoht, a Shēna who will do great things for all who share the title."

She looked like she had more to say but she just stopped and slowly closed her eyes.

"Grandma," I called, "Wake up! Please, wake up! You're all I have left!"

"She's gone," I heard a voice say from behind. I looked back and saw Morpheus with a fairly solemn face. "I didn't want to interrupt," he told me before walking away. "I suggest you go and bury her before you confront me again, out of respect of course."

I couldn't believe what he was saying. 'Out of *respect*'? He's the one who killed her! And I wasn't going to let him leave without paying for it. Even though I had no strength to fight I still stood up and ran, ready to claw at him with my one hand if I had to. But before I could reach him, he turned to me. Stretched out his hand and fired an attack that I had never seen him use before. I didn't know what it was. It didn't even feel like that power could come from someone like him. But I couldn't match up to it and in the end all I saw was darkness.

CHAPTER TWENTY-EIGHT
ALIZEH

I didn't know how long I was out for but I could barely move. And when I tried to, all I could feel was a numb pain. Aeson sat over me using his magic, giving my body a golden glow.

"Don't move," he told me. "You've got a few broken bones. We both used a little too much power. More than your body could handle. I'm too warn out to even fully heal you. The most I can do for you right now is numb the pain and work on healing you a bit more later."

"Thank you Aeson," I said before really focusing my eyes on him. "You look different." His hair was a bit longer. And he was taller than I originally thought.

"Oh yeah, that's just the drawback to *Steroeidés*. It uses a lot of my own *life force* to fuel it and ages me up a bit. I've never had to use it for so long before. If I had to guess, then it's probably aged me up by a year. Physically, I should be the same age as you now."

"Seriously? That's insane!" I sat up but quickly screamed in pain before laying right back down. Forgot about the broken bones. "Did that happen to me? Did I also get aged up too?"

"Probably a little bit. I had to draw from some of your own life force for that last attack. It probably aged you up by a few months. I'm sorry I didn't warn you."

"It's ok, I don't mind. If it wasn't for that spell then we would have both been dead. You helped save a lot of people today, Aeson. The cost doesn't matter."

Aeson blushed a little after I said that. It was kinda cute. Not as cute as Rai, but it made me smile.

I heard rustling not too far from us and saw Thelonious slowly crawling around beaten and bruised. It looked as if he was looking for something. Probably his wand. It seemed as if Aeson wasn't able to finish him off until he finally spoke to his brother.

"Don't even bother Thelonious," Aeson said to his brother while holding up the Earth Spirit Caster. "You lost."

Thelonious finally sat still. It wasn't graceful, but he finally accepted defeat. It looked like Aeson *was* able to end this without me.

"Why did you leave mom and me?" Aeson asked him. Thelonious didn't answer, allowing Aeson to continue, "We love you. *I* love you. You meant everything to me and you abandoned us for some foolish fairytale?" Thelonious looked away, refusing to look Aeson in the eyes. "That lack of empathy is exactly why you lost to us. A couple of children. And it's also the reason why you'll never deserve a Spirit Caster."

It was crazy to think how much one battle could change a person. Before I didn't think much of Aeson. He was kind but timid.

Small not only in appearance, but also in his personality and how he carried himself. But now Aeson was talking down to his own big brother like an adult. And I found that way too cool.

Finely Thelonious reacted. But it wasn't because of Aeson. He looked in an entirely different direction, shocked at another person's presence. I looked in the same direction and saw them. The two people that I had been looking for ever since I started this journey. It was Morpheus. And he was holding Arachne in his arms. She was covered in blood and I could barely feel any Rēa from her. She was dying.

"Thelonious," Morpheus said. "Go and get the girl from the runes and bring her up here."

Thelonious nodded his head, stumbled onto his feet and made his way down the mountain.

I didn't understand who he was referring to or what he was really making Thelonious do, but I didn't care. As he was giving the order I forced myself up to my feet despite the pain and shouted, "Morpheus! Where's my father? You both took him, didn't you? Don't even try to deny it!"

He was silent for a moment while he studied me. Something about him felt different but I couldn't tell what. He didn't beat around the bush with his answer like I thought he would.

"Yes, we took your father."

"Where is he? What did you do with him? What did you do with everyone you took?" I shouted at him.

"They're dead. Every last one of them," he told me dryly.

His words came as so much of a shock that I couldn't believe a single word. "No... you're lying!" I choked.

He stayed silent with an unamused look on his face. It looked as if he himself was grieving. I didn't understand why. Why was he lying? He had to be lying! I ran in his direction ready to beat the truth out of him.

As he was holding Arachne, he raised a finger towards me and a dark beam of energy shot right out of it and hit me straight in my chest. I felt it pierce all the way through like a bullet causing me to fall right back to the ground.

"Alizeh!" Aeson shouted while running to help me, but Morpheus stopped him by saying, "Don't move or your next." Aeson listened, too scared to share the same fate as me. Morpheus reassured him, "Don't worry, I didn't hit her heart. Whether she lives or dies is up to you." He walked past me and over to Aeson before finally placing Arachne on the ground in front of him. "Can you heal her?" he asked.

"I don't think so," Aeson answered, "That wound is too serious. It would take more than everything I have and would probably kill me before I could save her."

"Does it look like I care about what'll happen to you if you try?" He pointed his hand towards me, and it radiated dark energy. "You have until the count of three to heal Arachne or I'm killing Alizeh."

"Don't do it, Aeson. Let her die. You don't know the things she's done." I coughed.

"One," Morpheus counted.

"But if I don't then he'll kill you," Aeson argued.

"Then let *me* die!" I argued back.

"*Two*," Morpheus reminded him of his short time limit.

"Wait!" Aeson halted Morpheus. "I'll do it."

Morpheus lowered his hand and waited for Aeson to hold up his end of the deal. Aeson hesitantly went to work repairing the open wound. His body burst with light as he used all of his remaining power to do so. It didn't take long for Arachne to gasp for air and cling on to Morpheus as if he was life itself. Soon she was almost fully healed and Aeson fell face first to the ground, not moving a single inch. I didn't feel anything from him. It made me wonder if he truly did give his life to save Arachne's ... and in turn mine.

"Aeson?" I called, still unable to move from my injuries. "Aeson, get up!"

"How am I alive?" Arachne asked Morpheus.

"That doesn't matter. What matters is that you're still with us and we still have a mission that needs to be completed."

She looked confused but nodded her head. Morpheus got up and stretched his hand out making a black ball of fire not too far from them. It looked just like the portal that Kira used to escape from Phoenix Island. But how could he have possibly gained an ability like that? It didn't make any sense.

At the same time Thelonious finally came back up but with the last person I expected. It was Wren. She was passed out in his arms, but she was alive.

"Put her down," Morpheus ordered.

Thelonious did as he was told and then looked over at Aeson who was still motionless on the ground. "What did you do to Aeson?" he asked, seeming almost concerned for his younger brother's well being despite the fight to the death moments before.

"The same thing I'm going to do to you," Morpheus pointed his finger at him and shot him with the same attack he hit me with, forcing him to the ground in the same position as me. He tried to get up, but Morpheus stopped him by saying, "Don't you dare move Thelonious. Do you really think I didn't notice that stunt you pulled during this fight? You almost killed everyone in the area including Arachne and me. I have half a mind to finish you off."

He walked over to Thelonious and picked up Wren before turning to Arachne and saying, "Let's go."

"Where the hell do you think you're going, Morpheus! And where are you taking Wren?" I shouted.

"I *think* I'm going to stand upon the heavens. And this girl is going to be the key to that."

"Stop screwing with me!" I screamed, "Come back here and face me! Tell me where my father is!"

"It's like I told you before. He's dead. But if you're looking for his body then look downstairs. It'll be there along with everyone else you're looking for, including Rai."

"Wait, what did you do to Rai?" I tried to stand back up but still couldn't move an inch.

He avoided my question by saying, "Goodbye, Alizeh Green." And with that he walked through the portal with Wren and Arachne, and they were gone, closing the portal behind them.

I lost. Aeson was dying, I couldn't feel Rai's Rēa anywhere, Morpheus took Wren and I couldn't do a damn thing to stop him. If Morpheus was telling the truth ... if he was telling the truth about dad ... I didn't know what I would tell mom. That is if she even *survived* the poison. But an even more immediate problem was whether or not I'd even survive this simple chest wound. I was bleeding out. And I was cold. I couldn't move. My vision was getting blurry. I don't think I'm going to make it. And somehow, on top of all that, the worst part about my failure was not knowing what would come from it. Morpheus was still out there, and I could only hope that there was someone out there who could stop him.

CHAPTER TWENTY-NINE
FLINT

The citizens of Ebony all stood around in a crowd arguing with one another over how they should proceed with all the recent rumors that came to light. It seemed that everyone knew the truth. Or at least pieces of the truth; Kira having a part to play in the destruction of this city was definitely a big piece.

Delta walked up to me as I watched from a distance and asked, "What's going on?"

"Some of your fellow citizens have a problem with the person who's running things."

One of the men in the crowd turned and spotted Delta. He immediately left the crowd while calling her name, getting everyone's attention.

"Miss Mizuno! Delta Mizuno!" he called while heading in our direction. "Where is the Queen?"

Delta went to meet him halfway and answered, "Queen Kira is currently busy with her royal duties. But I can assist you."

"Do you know when she'll be available?"

"Unfortunately, no. She's not in the castle at the moment and I don't know when she'll be back."

"Well what's she doing?" Another person shouted from across the room.

"How can she not be here in a time like this?" A third person spoke.

"She needs to answer for what she's done! Where is she?"

Delta was overwhelmed by the flurry of questions but still had to come up with answers. I wasn't even sure if Delta herself knew that Kira was the cause of the city's destruction. She was silent for a moment before finally perking her lips to speak but something stopped her. The presence of Rēa erupting in the center of the great hall. It was black and wavy like a ball of dark flames. I remembered this spell. It was the same one that Kira and Delta used to leave Phoenix Island after their fight with Crystal. But this was strange. I could've sworn Kira lost her wand and yet I saw her spell being used before my very eyes. Delta looked just as confused from the new development. Everyone waited in suspense for their Queen to walk through the portal but unfortunately it wasn't her. Someone new was using the ability.

Morpheus walked out of the portal with Arachne walking out behind him while holding a small child in her arms. I'd never seen them before and had no idea why they'd have a young girl with them. But she was the least of our problems. Everyone was silent as he strolled through the hall like his presence was a disruption to us all.

"Please Delta," he finally said. "Don't let my entrance stop you from answering our fellow citizens. Where is the princess?" Delta stayed silent, just staring at him, still trying to process his sudden appearance but Morpheus pressed on. "Why isn't she here? Surely she must care about all of her loyal subjects in their time of need? Especially since she's the one who caused this disaster."

Those words caused a stir around the room. It wasn't a large stir, but it was enough to get people talking. He was a person in a position of power basically confirming every one's suspicions.

Delta leaned in close to him and said, "Morpheus, let's talk about this in private."

"Why? Surely these poor souls here deserve to know how we *really* came to this situation. Or do you plan on hiding the truth from them forever?" This created an even bigger stir that couldn't be swept under the rug. Everyone was waiting for Morpheus to continue, and he was happy to do so. He jumped onto a large table and announced, "I'm sure you're all curious. But before I say anything, do any of you know who I am?"

One man hesitantly stepped up and said, "Morpheus Morningstar, right? A member of the Five Armaments. You were believed to be dead."

"I almost died," he confirmed. "I was attacked by someone who I believed to be my ally. A fellow member of the Armaments and the only surviving member who currently isn't in this room."

This started a rise out of everyone in the room, but someone finally came to challenge his bold claims. "You lie!" a lone soldier argued. "Why would the Queen attack you?

"The same reason she attacked all of you. Surely some of you saw it? The monster she turned into?"

Ranne finally decided to intervene and walked over to the table Morpheus was standing on with a scowl on her face. "Morpheus, get off the table," she ordered.

"Ahh, has the princess's *sword* come to silence me?" he mocked.

"I came to put an end to your lies."

"He's not lying!" someone yelled. Everyone looked back at the small child who had been following Kira around ever since I got here. It was Kian. "I saw it with my own eyes! She turned into a monster and destroyed everything. She even killed my mother!"

I personally was shocked to hear this information come from the kid. Did this kid really know about Kira's transformation or was he lying? And if so, then why would he have stayed so close to Kira, the woman who supposedly killed his mother. Either way this was a setup regardless of whether or not he was telling the truth.

"I think he's telling the truth," one woman came out to say. "He's not the first person to say that."

"The entire royal bloodline is filled with demons. What would make Kira so different?" another man pointed out.

"She's a monster! She did this to us!"

"Where is she? Where is the Queen?" They shouted in an uproar. Guards came to calm people down but that only made everyone more on edge, driving some to the point of violence.

Arachne finally pulled herself onto the table and shouted, "I say we raise hell until we find the princess and make her answer for her crimes!"

Ranne quickly jumped up on the table and shouted back, "You will do no such thing! And anyone who even speaks another word of it will be arrested for treason!"

Morpheus got in between them and asked Ranne, "Do you really think you can stop me?"

"Easily," she answered with a red glow to her eyes. She then grabbed his wrist tight so he couldn't reach his Spirit Caster. But he didn't need it. He used a dark magic that none of us saw coming and with a flick of his wrist, there was black.

A dark energy wave blasted Ranne off the table and across the room, knocking the wind out of her. Everyone was shocked at this new power. A dark aura emanated from his body as he looked around at everyone in the room.

"What are you all waiting for? Find Kira! I won't let any harm come to those who seek justice!"

Some people hesitated but most were already riled up and used the momentum to do exactly as Arachne had suggested. *Raise hell.* They attacked every guard they could see, and some rioters were even able to overpower them and take their weapons, turning this into an even fight.

Morpheus hopped off the table and made his way towards Delta, but she was still too shocked to move.

"How did you do that?" she shuddered. "You've never shown power like this before."

He raised his hand, admiring the dark sparks flickering off of it. "Oh this? This is something entirely new. Ya know, out of all the Five Armaments I've always wondered which of us were the strongest. I had my theory that it was either you or Kira. If she weren't so mentally weak then it would've been an easy pick. Now that I have her powers in my hand I can test that theory."

"Don't do this, Morpheus," Delta pleaded to the lost cause.

Without warning, Morpheus raised his hand and hit Delta with the same attack he used against Ranne but this time it was stronger. Delta went flying through the air and crashed through the wall and out of the castle. Morpheus followed her through the broken wall.

It looked like things were getting complicated. I couldn't stand on the sidelines anymore. I took a deep breath, trying to muster whatever Rēa I had left to burst from my body, but it was a failure. I hadn't recovered even a spec of Rēa since my battle with the king. It made me wonder if I'd ever get my power back. But I couldn't let that stop me. I had to help in any way I could.

I ran after them and found myself entering the courtyard. Morpheus had his hand up to hit Delta with another blast, but I stopped him before he could do so by swinging my Spirit Caster at the back of his head. But the attack didn't do anything. He was prepared and already had his defenses up. If anything, the only reason he even stopped his attack against Delta was simply because he was annoyed by me.

I went in for another swing but this time Morpheus caught my wand before it could hit him and said, "Stop it. You really think you can beat me with a stick? Are you trying to insult me? Unless ..." he let go of my wand and looked me up and down "I don't sense any Rēa coming from you. That's *interesting*. You were the strongest of Crystal's faction, but now you seem to have become the weakest. You're the only one of her friends I haven't killed and I was dreading the thought of having to take you on. But now things should go a lot smoother."

"*Killed*? What do you mean *'killed'*?" I asked, unable to believe what he was saying.

"Well I guess *kill* might be an exaggeration. I didn't deliver any finishing blows but Alizeh Green and Rai Leoht are currently laying in a puddle of their own blood on the other side of the continent. Oh, and Ana is already buried."

"Y-you're lying!"

"I know it must be hard to accept. You were fond of that one, weren't you? Well don't worry, you'll be joining them soon enough."

He then blasted me into the dirt. For a moment I couldn't breathe from the impact. And I could barely move. Without Rēa I couldn't take attacks like I used to. He raised his hand over me to finish me off but stopped once he heard a spell being formed behind him.

"Chtapódi."

Morpheus turned to see Delta surrounded in a small bubble of water. Eight tentacle-like whips shot out of the bubble on all sides looking like they were ready to strike. All the water together seemed to resemble the shape of a giant octopus that surrounded her body.

Morpheus turned his attack from me and instead shot the blast at Delta. It hit her dead on, creating a puff of black smoke around her but once it left it looked like there wasn't even a scratch on her. This was the same thing I went through the last time I fought her.

"As per usual you found the perfect way to defend yourself. That mixed with your intellect is what makes you so dangerous," Morpheus commended.

Delta didn't thank him. She used one of the whips to attack him, but he was able to dodge it. She then attacked with the rest of them striking one by one from every angle, but he still was able to just narrowly avoid every attack. That's a feat I don't think even I could've done at full power. The first time I fought Morpheus wasn't a long enough fight to fully gouge his abilities, but I know for a fact that he was never this fast. Not only did he get a new power, but he was faster and likely stronger. I could only assume that facet of his body was enhanced, but I couldn't tell what the scope of his new power was.

Soon the tentacles surrounded him and wrapped around his body, completely trapping him. Delta lifted him into the air and smashed him against the castle walls. She kept him steady and then started grinding him into the wall like chalk before throwing him across the courtyard.

I don't know many people who would've gotten up from that but somehow Morpheus did. And other than a few scratches, he seemed almost completely fine. Like he could go on for hours. An explosion of black Rēa emanated from his body.

"Damnit," Delta cursed to herself. "He can take a lot more damage than before. How the hell did he get so strong?"

"You got my clothes dirty," Morpheus said before ripping off his cloak. He had black tattoos all over his chest but the strange part about them was that they seemed to have been glowing. "I can finally feel it," he continued. "This power is finally starting to become my own. Are you ready to see what I'm capable of? Because I'm curious myself."

He let out his power, causing a large number of black spheres to appear around him. And with the command, "Fire!" they each shot off a barrage of bullets that were able to push Delta's defense to its limit. At first they did nothing but after a few seconds they started to pierce through her protective bubble. It was too much for her to handle.

She stretched one of her tendrils up to the top of the castle walls and yanked herself up to get out of the bullets' path, but Morpheus wasn't going to let her escape. He jumped up high enough to scale the wall which completely shocked me. It seemed as if he had gained the ability to fly. Even if he had only made the jump from pure strength or Rēa it still had terrifying repercussions.

Once he landed on top of the wall, Delta wasted no time attacking. She whipped her tentacles at him but this time he didn't dodge. He blocked them. He then ran towards her, blocking and smacking every attack away until he was finally close enough to grab her.

At first, I thought any attack he would make would be fruitless from the strength of her shield, but he proved me wrong. Morpheus tore right through her defensive bubble, grabbed her by the neck and ripped her out of the water beast she had created. She was the heart and with her gone, the octopus melted and splattered everywhere turning into a simple puddle.

Morpheus still had her by the neck in the air and asked, "Please don't tell me you're done already? I'm still not done testing my power."

"I'm sorry," she choked. "I don't think I have any spells powerful enough to hurt you... so I'll just have to *drown* you. ***Ylakí Neroú!***"

Suddenly all the water that surrounded their feet gathered into the air and formed a bubble around both of them."

I thought that had to be it. She had him right where she wanted him. When she tried to drown me, it took everything I had to escape. But it was much easier for Morpheus.

He let out a large explosion that destroyed the water prison and broke part of the castle wall, forcing it to collapse. Delta was sent flying to the ground and crashed in a ditch. She was out cold.

Morpheus remained unscathed while floating down rather pleased with himself. "It seems there isn't a single Shēna on this plane of existence that can contend with me."

As soon as he landed Ranne came from behind and swung a sword right at the back of Morpheus's neck. For any normal being it would've been a fatal blow. Even for Shēna if they didn't see it coming. Attacking right at the moment of his victory should've been his most vulnerable moment, but he still had his defenses up and the blade didn't leave a scratch.

He looked back at Ranne with an unamused look which made her step a few paces back in fear.

"What the hell are you?" she shuddered.

"A God," he answered. "Now bow."

He pointed his finger at her leg and shot a thin beam of energy that pierced through it, forcing her to scream and take a knee to the ground just like he wanted. He then walked away seemingly done with the both of them. Arachne walked over my body as I was still unable to move, probably from a few broken bones.

Once she got close to him, she asked, "Are you done yet?"

"Yes," he answered. "That battle jolted my new powers awake. We can leave now." He turned towards the castle and called, "Kian! You can come out now!"

The young boy scurried through the broken castle wall and went to Morpheus asking, "Is it time brother?"

Brother? They were related? Is that why Kian had been following us around this whole time. Was he just some sort of spy that Morpheus used against us? But what was his purpose?

"Yes," Morpheus answered. "Did you find the gateway?"

Kian nodded.

"Then take us to it."

"Wait!" I shouted, still unable to move. "What the hell happened to you? You weren't this powerful back in our last battle. Crystal was able to beat you easily! How did you get so powerful in such a short amount of time?"

Morpheus stopped and said, "Well I guess I have you to thank for that."

"What the hell are you talking about?"

To answer my question, Morpheus pulled out his Illusion Spirit Caster and instantly changed his appearance. It was that of an old man whose face seemed vaguely familiar.

"Do you remember this face?" he asked.

I remembered that voice. I knew where I had seen this man. He was the one who bought those Phoenix feathers off me some time ago.

"I sold them to *you*? Is that how you got so powerful? You used the power from the feathers to become stronger?"

Morpheus discarded the illusion going back to his original form and told me, "Well it's a little more complicated than that, but I wouldn't want to bore you with the details. All you need to know is that obtaining these feathers was a necessary step in my evolution and I couldn't have done it without you. As a token of my appreciation, I'll let you live. It's not like you pose much of a threat to anyone now. Goodbye Flint Zapalac."

Then he and his allies disappeared out of sight. I couldn't believe how strong he had gotten. And it was all my fault. Rai ... Alizeh ... *Ana*. If he was telling the truth, then... if she truly was dead. Then it was because of me. I killed her just like I killed my past lover, Summer. And from the looks of it she wasn't the only one who was going to suffer that fate. I don't know what he's after but I know where he's headed. And Crystal will be waiting there. She's the last person standing between Morpheus and his goal and I prayed that she'd be able to stop him. No. That would be impossible. At this point I didn't even know if she'd survive. That's all she needed to do. Just survive and come back. We need her alive if we ever have a hope of beating him.

CHAPTER THIRTY
CRYSTAL

Kira and I walked through the doors of Reshma's shop hoping that our clothes would be finished by now.

"Reshma!" Kira called, "Aleron said you wanted to see us."

Reshma came from the back with two black boxes adorned with golden ribbons. "Do you know how long I've been waiting for you two?" she complained.

"We came as soon as you summoned us," I argued.

"Then you both walk slower than my worms can crawl," she criticized before passively throwing both boxes at us. "Now go in the back and try those on so I can gaze upon my creations on their new hosts."

Once she said that, I realized she wasn't trying to be rude. She was just excited to see us wear her newest creations. This was her art.

Kira and I did as we were told and went in the back into two separate rooms to try on the clothes. When I unraveled the present and opened the box, what I saw inside made me flinch. Whatever was in there was moving as if it were alive. But only slightly.

I pulled it out and it stopped. It made me wonder if I had just imagined it. Either way what I pulled out were just normal clothes, so regardless I had to put them on if I didn't want Reshma chewing me out again.

Once they were on, I walked out to show Reshma, while telling her, "It's a perfect fit."

"Of course it is," she told me while pulling me by the arm over to a giant mirror that covered one of the walls of her shop.

I was wearing a black almost skintight bodysuit with white fur boots. Over the suit, was a long white trench coat with fur on the trim of its hood and wrist. The fur was blue and flowed like fire even though there wasn't a draft to help it do so. It was as if the material itself was alive.

"What is this?" I asked while grabbing a few strands. Touching it gave me a similar feeling to when I touch a Spirit Caster. There was a small surge of energy. Of life.

"Fur from the Ice Capra," she answered. "I don't believe you have those where you come from. I guess you can liken them to goats. It was the first thing I thought of when I saw you."

"You thought of a goat when you saw me?"

"Around here they're a symbol for maturity, leadership, and intense motivation. That's the vibration I got from your aura."

That was the first compliment she gave me since I got to this dimension.

Kira cut through our conversation with a heavy clang from her new metallic boot. We both turned to see her wearing a black dress covered in armor. Specifically a sleek chest plate, sharpened gauntlets and boots with armored greaves that reached farther up her dress than I could see. Every piece of armor was engraved with red roses that stretched out like vines.

"I was expecting something a little more formal," said Kira. "This seems like something that's more suited towards battle."

"Well, you are a ruler are you not?" Reshma asked. "There will be times where you'll be diplomatic and then there are times when you'll need to go to war. I made you something that you can do both in. I think it fits well with your current goals. You want to be a better ruler? One that's better than your predecessors, right?"

Kira gave a more serious face and looked at herself in the mirror. She fixed her posture and answered back, "Yes, that's right."

I looked down at my coat and noticed a golden rose on the left breast. It was similar to one of the many roses that adorned Kira's armor.

"You like it?" Reshma asked. "It's my insignia. Anyone who sees you wearing it will practically worship you for wearing one of my pieces."

I couldn't tell if she was just stroking her own ego, but still her explanation did put a smile on my face. Regardless, I knew these clothes were special.

"And you wanna see the best part?" she continued.

"What is it?" I asked.

Reshma proceeded to take out a pair of scissors from her pocket before saying, "Brace yourself."

"What?" I asked, not fully understanding the command.

Before I could fully brace myself, she jabbed the scissors right into my gut forcing me to freeze. Even Kira had a look of terror on her face. But once Reshma pulled back, I realized that I didn't feel any pain. The blades didn't pierce me. And my clothes didn't even have a scratch on them. Reshma showed me the scissors and they had shattered into pieces.

"This fabric is almost indestructible, at least by your world's standards," she explained. "There aren't many beings or artifacts that can tear it. And if somehow you do manage to get it damaged then you can always come back to me to fix it. For a price of course."

"Whatever the price is, it'll be worth it to keep these new gifts," Kira grinned.

"Thank you Reshma," I concluded.

"Anytime darling," she turned away from us. "You two should get a move on. I hear Abraham's pretty excited to give *his* gift out to you, Kira. Don't keep him waiting."

***

We walked into Abraham's forge and saw him holding a wand that looked like it was made entirely out of glass. But other than that, there didn't seem to be anything out of the ordinary with it.

Abraham turned to us, surprised at our sudden appearance and greeted us.

"Kira! Crystal! It's good to see the both of you."

"It's good to see you too," Kira greeted back. "Did you finish the wand?"

"Just about. I'm going to need your help with putting the finishing touches on it."

"I'm sorry, did you say *my* help?" she was taken aback.

"Yes, *your* help. Now come and stand right here for a moment."

Kira hesitantly walked over to him while arguing, "But I've never made anything in my life."

"I know. That's why we're going to whip those dainty little hands into shape. Now hold this."

He handed her the wand.

"What do I do with it?" she asked.

Abraham walked away from her while saying, "Just hold it high above your head and don't move."

She did exactly as she was told and asked, "Like this?"

Abraham walked over to a strange machine that I had never seen before. There were blinking buttons that he typed away on and a lever that he held on to tight. He looked back up at her and said, "Yes Kira, just like that. Now make sure you brace yourself and *don't* let go of that wand. It'll be the only thing stopping the beam from cutting you right in half."

Kira stopped and stared at Abraham trying to wrap her mind around what he just told her to do and the consequences to the smallest slip up.

"What?" she finally asked.

"Don't worry, that's just the worst-case scenario," he reassured her as he pulled the lever. A large machine wrapped in metal and glass started to glow above Kira's head charging up a massive amount of Rēa. "The best-case scenario is that you'll just explode," he continued.

"Wait... *what?*"

Kira had no time to react. A beam of light shot down from the machine and impacted the wand in Kira's hands with enough force to almost push *me* over. And I wasn't even standing that close. I couldn't even imagine what Kira had to go up against.

"*What. The actual. Hell!*" Kira screamed as she struggled to stay on her feet.

"Are you alright Kira?" Abraham shouted over the reverberating sound of the clash.

"This is ... intense!" she answered. "Every bone in my body ... feels like it's going to explode. It hurts. I can't hold this!"

"Well, you'll have to hold it because the alternative is death."

All I could feel was a tremendous amount of heat. If it were me, I would have let go a long time ago. But Kira was holding on. Her will was still intact but starting to shatter.

I quickly made my way to Abraham while asking, "What is all this?"

"We're fueling her Spirit Caster with its elemancy," he answered. "I'm experimenting with energy I got from a dying star."

The energy forced Kira down to her knees as she screamed, "It burns!" Tears and sweat rushed down her face.

"Abraham, she's going to die!" I warned him.

"If you don't think she can handle it then maybe you should help her."

"By doing *what* exactly?"

"She said it burns. Maybe you should cool her off?"

I didn't waste any time assisting her. I ran over to her and shouted, **"*Droserós!*"** The spell was supposed to cool down the area but it wasn't doing much in the face of this heat. I put more power into it while shouting to raise my power. The area instantly froze over. I had the wand pointed at Kira's hands, but the ice melted before it could even form.

"You'll have to do better than that Crystal!" Abraham shouted at me from a distance. "Give it everything you've got or Kira's as good as dead! Hell, you'll probably die from that distance as well!"

"I can't!" I shouted back. The heat was too much.

"If you can't save yourself and Kira, then how do you ever plan to save your sister?"

Those words made me snap. He was right. I couldn't die here. And I couldn't let anyone else die either. I was too strong to be stopped by something like this. And I had to be stronger to save Wren.

I pushed beyond my limits and envisioned a power that could match this. Me at my strongest. I remembered my battle against The King.

Suddenly my Spirit Caster changed just like it did on that day. It evolved. My power was bolstered. The room froze covering the walls and floor in ice.

"That's it Crystal! Keep the temperature just like that!" Abraham encouraged. "Now Kira, I need you to put all of your Rēa into that wand. Fuel it with every last drop."

"Alright," Kira huffed as she slowly got back up to her feet. There was a sharp surge of power that emanated from her and went straight up into the wand. The stream of energy stopped raining down and with its disappearance, came another burst of light that exploded from the wand, sweeping me off my feet.

But Kira was still standing there with the brilliant wand still in her hands far above her head. The light almost created a full halo over her making her look angelic for a moment. Steam rose from her body as if the blood within her veins had boiled from the task.

"Kira," I called. "Are you ok?"

Even though the energy beam was gone, she still wept. But I don't think it was because of the pain. It was something different.

"I... I feel whole again," she sobbed.

"Bravo!" Abraham cut in, applauding us. "That was excellent teamwork. I feel like we all really bonded in that exercise.

Kira wiped away her tears and glared over at him with a menacing look that I haven't seen from her since our last battle in Ebony.

"Abraham," she growled while stalking her way towards him. "I'm going to kill you for that."

"Now why would you want to go and do a thing like that?" he asked as if he genuinely didn't have a clue. "I gave you exactly the kind of experience you've been yearning for."

"What the hell are you on about?"

"You wanted to suffer, did you not?"

Those words made Kira stop in place.

"You didn't even think you deserved that wand because of your past sins. So, I let you suffer to prove yourself. Not many people could have endured what you just went through. Think of it as a right of passage."

Kira calmed down and took a good look at her new wand, seemingly satisfied with his answer and asked, "Why is it white? And it's so damn bright. It kinda clashes with its whole dark aesthetic, don't you think?"

"That's because it has nothing to do with darkness. What you're holding is the *Light* Spirit Caster. It's not too different from your old one. In fact, it has just as much free will."

"So it imprints on its users, just like the Dark Spirit Caster?"

"Precisely. The only difference is that *you* are its first wielder. Your actions will dictate its growth and how it will affect future users. Welcome to parenthood!"

Kira didn't respond. She was glaring hard at her new Spirit Caster. She had a whole new weight on her shoulders; to be an example.

Abraham turned to me and said, "I see that you successfully evolved your Spirit Caster during our little exercise."

Once he reminded me, I lit up and looked down at my Spirit Caster, but it had already reverted back to its original form. The sight made me deflate.

"No," I said flatly, "it was just a fluke."

"It would appear that way, wouldn't it?" he asked with a hefty smile.

"Do you know something I don't?" I asked hoping that he saw my situation differently.

"A lot actually, young one," he boasted. "But this is a strange occurrence. You're an enigma Ms. Winters. You might unlock your full potential in ten years, or you might unlock it tomorrow. It just depends on your will."

Kira was finally done admiring her wand and went to shake his hand, "Thank you for this. I don't know how to repay such a debt."

"You can repay it by being a good influence on that wand. That's the only thing I'll ever ask of you," he told her as he grabbed her open hand and shook it.

"Consider it done."

I decided to cut in with an important question. "Before we leave, I need to ask you something."

"What is it?" he asked.

"The other day, you said that Alizeh and Rai were on a collision course with Morpheus. What happened? Did they collide?"

"I'm not sure. Let me check." He closed his eyes and looked around as if they were open. His investigation was silent. And uncomfortably long. When he finally opened his eyes, the next words that came out of his mouth was the worst-case scenario that I didn't want to hear.

"They lost."

"What?" I asked in disbelief.

"They all lost. Every last one of your allies have lost in battle against Morpheus."

"Every single one? Even Ana and Flint?"

"Yes. All of them."

That got Kira's attention.

"Wait, but Flint was in Ebony," Kira explained. "Did Morpheus go to the castle? Are Ranne and Delta ok?"

"It's like I said," he continued to explain to us with the same words. "They *all* lost."

"We need to go back *right now*!" I protested while storming towards the door. "Kira, we're leaving."

"There's no need." he advised us.

"And why's that?" asked Kira.

"Because he found his way to us."

The same sirens that blared when we first entered this dimension activated once again but this time it wasn't for us. Abraham dropped to his knees while the alarms wailed and started praying. I wondered if it was out of fear. And what god he could have possibly been praying to. That question was answered with the sudden appearance of a familiar face.

The Cosmic Queen of this dimension appeared right in between Kira and I. It was almost instantaneous, as if she had appeared from thin air. Kira and I jumped at the sight of her.

"If you're summoning me here then I can only assume we have a real threat on our hands," she spoke.

"Potentially, yes," Abraham answered. "I'm requesting that you take Crystal and Kira under your care. If they go outside to face this threat, then they'll most certainly die."

"So, you want me to protect your favorites?"

"They have too much potential to fall here," he explained.

"As you wish. I will protect them for now." She turned to us and continued, *"You two are coming with me."*

"Wait—" I tried to plead but I was too slow. We had instantly left the room and were forced into another against our will. "Where are we?"

"The throne room," Kira answered, just as confused as I was. "But how?"

"I teleported you both here," The Queen echoed.

"You brought us here to hide?" I asked. "I don't want to hide. I want to fight! I need to find my sister and the only person who knows where she is, is right on your doorstep!"

"Calm yourself Crystal. You heard what Abraham said. You're not ready for this fight. Neither of you are."

"So you want me to just do *nothing*? Last time I did nothing, people died! My *family* died!"

"And if you go out there right now, you'll die. Trust me Crystal. My people will defeat Morpheus. And I will personally find out where he is keeping your sister. Even if I have to rip the memory from his corpse."

CHAPTER THIRTY-ONE
ARACHNE

I had to watch my step to make sure I didn't step in a pool of blood or trip over a dismembered arm. The two men who were standing in front of us, ready to attack just moments ago were reduced to nothing but filleted pieces of flesh. I didn't expect Morpheus to use such a brutal attack.

"I'm sorry for the mess," he told us. "I didn't mean to kill them."

"Looks like you don't know your own strength," I suggested while never taking my eyes off the bodies.

"Well that's not entirely untrue. I'm much stronger now than I was before when I fought Delta."

"What?" I finally looked up at him. "How's that possible? It hasn't even been fifteen minutes since that battle happened."

Morpheus looked as if he was thinking of an answer but soon turned his attention to Kian who was having a hard time breathing. I guessed it was from the dead bodies. Must've been too much for the poor kid.

Morpheus got down on one knee and said, "Kian, hop on my back. I'll carry you the rest of the way."

"I'm sorry Morpheus." Kian huffed as he latched onto Morpheus. "I don't know what's wrong with me."

"Don't apologize Kian, it's not your fault. Your body's just having a difficult time adjusting to this dimension. I can't explain it but something about the air here feels different. To you it must feel heavy, but to me it feels familiar in more ways than one."

"Is that a good thing?" I asked.

"I feel like I'm in my element and it's intoxicating. Now come. It's time to see how far I can push my new strength."

Kian nodded his head, and Morpheus carried him on his back while I followed with Wren still in my arms. We walked through the halls for some time until we finally discovered a hall with steps that led upwards. This had to be an exit.

We walked up steps and outside of the building. The structures around us were golden and the sky above us was a sea of colors. Unfortunately, I couldn't focus on any of that because there was a small army of soldiers who were waiting for us and blocked our way. Each one of them had a spear pointing in our direction.

One dark skinned man stood before them with a commanding presence and asked us, "Who are you and what purpose do you have stepping foot in *our* dimension?"

Morpheus stepped up with Kian still on his back and answered back in a just as commanding voice, "My name is Morpheus Morningstar and I came here to claim my spot on the throne."

"*Your* spot on the throne? What right would a foreigner have to our world?"

"It's my birthright. A promised gift from the god who left this world long ago. My mother, and your formal ruler, *Amaranth*."

Any doubts that I had before were put to rest from all the constant mutters that every single soldier went into. Even the one in front gained a new expression on his face. One of surprise. But he was still able to keep his cool.

"Get on your knees and put your hands behind your head," he ordered. "If you comply then we will alert Queen Céleste of your presence so that she can personally decide your fate."

"And if I refuse?"

His words gave me a chill. Morpheus was in control, and everyone knew it. I could see it from the tense looks on the soldiers' faces. Although the Commander who was speaking to us didn't seem to get that same chill.

"Then *I* will decide your fate, here and now. And I'm not as merciful as the Queen."

I could feel Morpheus's Rēa rising farther than I had ever felt it before. He didn't need to say anything for everyone to get the message. He wasn't going to submit.

"I'll take my chances."

The Commander scoffed and gave the order to his men, "Take him down," They all hesitated but still obeyed while closing in around us.

Morpheus rolled his neck as if he were about to take on a warm up before the real workout and whispered to Kian, "Hold on tight." He then stretched out his hand, allowing a stream of dark energy to shoot out of it and swiped it to his right to slice through the five soldiers to his right. He stretched all five fingers on his left hand and shot a thin dark beam out of each tip to pierce through five more soldiers on his left side.

Blue beams of energy rained down from nearby towers scattered about, all aimed at Morpheus and Kian. He waved his hand over his head to create a black shield that forced the blasts to bounce and ricochet away.

Once the archers realized hitting him was a fruitless task, some seemed to aim their sights towards me. With Wren still in my arms I wasn't quick enough to get out of the way but Morpheus took quick note of that. With another wave of his hand he created a large black dome around us so that we didn't get hit. He then flew up in the air going almost as fast as the small girl I fought back in Ebony and shot a blast towards one of the towers, causing its top to explode and kill whatever archers were in it. He then flew higher and shot more energy blasts in every direction to do the same to the other towers, destroying them one by one. Soon there wasn't a single arrow being shot.

Once he was done with that he decided to turn his attention back to the foot soldiers. He balled his fist and focused all Rēa into it before flying back down to the middle of the crowd and punching the ground beneath them, causing a major shockwave that pushed everyone away from him. But that only made the ones who were farther, push towards him like a wave.

"It's like lambs to the slaughter!" Morpheus laughed wildly as he waved his arms around with dark energy flowing from them. He sliced through soldier after soldier, tearing each one apart. With every blast, every scream, and every death, it became more and more apparent that nothing would stop him.

"Everyone stand down!" The Commander shouted.

Everyone stopped in place. Even Morpheus calmed his manic frenzy. The man walked up to him as every soldier cleared a path for them to talk face to face.

"You're giving up already?" Morpheus asked with a large grin. "A wise choice. You finally recognize me as your new god."

"I recognize you as a *threat* that no average man can overcome," The Commander corrected him. "Unfortunately for you, I'm no average man."

His eyes flashed an intense crimson after the statement that left Morpheus in an almost shocked state. Not one of fear but more of wonder.

"Those eyes..." Morpheus started to say. "You're a Zubarian. I've seen what your race is capable of. You're fearsome to most but you don't scare me."

"Really now? Let's fix that."

Suddenly his long black locks and beard started to fade until they were completely white. White blotches formed on his face and down his neck. They weren't random. It was a design of some sort. Like tribal tattoos from a race forgotten by time. And without any hesitation, he drew his sword and slashed at Morpheus. Morpheus was too slow to react and got a good cut right on his chest. It was only after the cut that he had the sense to leap away from the man and back over to Wren and I, basically retreating into the bubble with us.

"Morpheus, are you ok?" I asked.

"This man," Morpheus took a deep breath, "he's different. I've never seen any Zubarian as fast as that. I can't even fathom what his strength must be like. Kian. Get off. Now."

Kian listened and let go, trying to stand on his own two feet but still ended up falling down. He still couldn't bear the energy in this realm. But his needs had to be tossed aside for now. And he knew that.

"Be careful brother," Kian told him.

"I'll try. Just make sure you two stay out of the way. If you get too close to us, I don't think I'll be able to protect you."

"Don't worry," I assured him. "I'll keep Kian close."

"Are you giving up already?" The Commander shouted at us from beyond the bubble. "I thought you were supposed to convince me that you were my god?"

Morpheus dispersed the dome and started to make his way back over to the man while saying, "Oh, I'm still going to convince you. I just needed to discard a little weight to prove it."

"Sounds good to me. I would've killed you with that first strike, but I didn't want that child to get caught in it. Don't think I'm going to hold back again."

"I love that chivalry," Morpheus laughed. "What's your name, soldier?"

"Aleron; Living Sword of Céleste."

"That's an intimidating title, *Aleron*. After I take over this dimension, I might just keep you around as one of my personal soldiers."

Aleron was done talking. Once Morpheus was in range, Aleron once again drew his sword faster than I could process and aimed straight for his head, but Morpheus was able to duck backwards and once again jump away to gain a little bit of distance. The only difference was that it didn't take him long to jump back into the fight. A burst of dark energy formed around his right hand making something in the vein of a sword. He dashed towards Aleron and their blades clashed.

Morpheus dashed all around him, attacking from all angles in ways I had never seen him move before. Regardless of the impressive performance, it still didn't put an ounce of pressure onto Aleron. He blocked every attack while never moving from his original spot. It's like he wasn't even trying. He was the first person to give Morpheus any *real* trouble since he gained his new abilities. And he wasn't even a Shēna. He was technically just some glorified gatekeeper. At this point I couldn't imagine who else we'd have to face in this dimension.

Morpheus leaped back. Melee combat wasn't going to work on this guy, so Morpheus decided to go for another approach. He gaped his mouth wide and in its center was a small blast of energy. The attack was identical to Kira's when she went into that monstrous form.

With a loud shout he fired it right at Aleron. The beam enveloped him with enough power that would destroy someone like me. But this man wasn't anything like me. He was a *monster*.

Once the dust cleared the only thing turned to dust was his chest armor. I could see his massively toned body and the white tattoos that accompanied. They looked just like the ones on his face.

"You done?" he asked, completely unfazed by the attack.

"That's impossible," Morpheus blurted. "What the hell are you?"

Aleron didn't waste any time answering the question. Instead, he charged at Morpheus. Morpheus tried to leap out of the way but Aleron was too fast. With one quick motion Aleron drove his blade right through Morpheus's chest.

They both stopped and stood there. Everyone who watched was silent. To them it must've looked like Aleron had won. But I know my Morpheus. He'd never go down so easily.

Morpheus's body started to crack like a mirror and eventually shattered to dust. It was an illusion. But before Aleron could fully process what had happened, Morpheus appeared right behind him and stabbed him right in his back.

I expected a look of shock or pain, but Aleron just looked confused. And he didn't grunt in pain. He simply asked, "How?"

"I'm the master of illusions my friend," he grinned. "I switched out right after I blasted you with that attack."

"Is that so? Well since I can actually *feel* this blade passing through me then that must mean *you're* the real one.

And without wasting another second he slashed his sword right at Morpheus, this time actually hitting the right one and making another deep wound on his chest.

Morpheus jumped back gaining distance, but it was obviously too late.

"Did you think that you'd really get the upper hand on me with these petty tricks?" Aleron huffed with a bead of sweat falling from his brow. "You obviously have no idea what you're up against."

Morpheus touched his wound and examined the blood. It was a serious gash, but he quickly regained his composure and looked back at Aleron with a smile.

"Neither do you."

Aleron heard a thud nearby and looked at the source. It was one of his soldiers. They had fallen right to the ground even though no one had even touched them. But that man wasn't the only one. It was his entire army. They were all dropping like flies.

And it didn't take long for Aleron to fall to his knees as well.

"What's happening to me?" he asked aloud. "This wound should be nothing."

My poison was finally kicking in. Morpheus told me to release it before we went into the portal just in case we had to deal with a threat like this. But doing this for so long was taxing. I was glad that this guy was finally going down so I could take a break.

Morpheus raised his hand towards him, charging another blast.

"Tell me," Morpheus said while standing above him, "do you recognize me as your god yet?"

Aleron didn't answer. He tried to get back up to his feet, but my poison made it impossible for him. This was finally going to be his end.

"Hm, not even a single final word? Have it your way."

Just as Morpheus was about to blast him away, a dark-skinned woman with the same white markings on her face as Aleron appeared beside him and grabbed Morpheus by his wrist, holding him tight so that he was forced to halt his attack.

She was so fast that Morpheus didn't see her coming. Hell, *I* didn't even notice her coming and I can currently see much more of the battlefield than he can.

Morpheus looked at her and his entire demeanor changed from calm and collected to tense and maybe a little annoyed.

"Who the hell are you?"

CHAPTER THIRTY-TWO
KIRA

○

Explosions could be heard every so often from the outside. Crystal paced back and forth across the throne room while I sat on the throne steps trying my best to not show how much I was internally freaking out.

"Crystal, can you please sit down?" I asked. "You're making me feel uneasy."

"You *should* feel uneasy!" she shouted back. "How can you be so calm in a time like *this*? We literally have no idea what's going on out there!"

"I'm *not* calm," I argued, "I'm barely holding it together right now. I wish we knew what was going on out there too, but that's just not going to happen right now."

"It can happen if that's what you both desire," Céleste interjected.

"Are you saying that you're finally going to let us out of here?" asked Crystal.

"No. But I can give you a similar experience."

Suddenly the stars that stretched around her body burst from her skin and surrounded us like dust. The stars made our entire surroundings change. I could see Morpheus standing in front of us. And Reshma was standing right beside him, holding his arm in place.

"Morpheus?" I called.

"He can't hear you. I am merely just showing you a vision. This is currently what's happening on the battlefield. You can watch but nothing more."

I paid close attention to the battle.

"Are you ok my love?" Reshma asked Aleron while holding onto Morpheus.

"I've been better," he answered. "What took you so long?"

"Unhand me!" Morpheus shouted over them trying his best to escape her grasp but she ignored him like a mother would with an unruly child.

"We were summoned by Abraham," she answered Aleron before pointing off to the side. "Apparently that girl who's been hiding over there has a Poison Spirit Caster. It's probably the reason you're in the state that you're in now.

I looked over and saw Arachne. So it was true. They *were* working together. But something even more interesting was the fact that she was holding Crystal's sister in her arms. Although her body was limp.

Crystal didn't take her eyes off of her.

"Wren ..." she muttered to herself. "Is she ..."

"She's alive," Céleste said to put her at ease. But she still looked tense and didn't take her eyes off her and Arachne. I knew that look. I haven't seen it since the last time Crystal tried to kill me.

I turned my attention back to the main fight.

"Anyways," Reshma continued. "Abraham made sure to give us immunity from her poison."

"*Us?* Aleron asked, knowing he wasn't a part of that immunity. "So I'm guessing the others are coming?"

"No." She chuckled. "They're already here darling."

Morpheus had enough of being ignored. He put his hand up and pointed it right at her face, charging an energy beam that looked like it had the power to take her head off. Before he could shoot it off Sage leaped in between them and smacked his hand away with his Spirit Caster while simultaneously causing an explosion to send Morpheus flying.

Before he could land on his feet, Reshma ran to him faster than he could react and punched him up into the air with unimaginable power. As he flew upward something shot towards him and grabbed him by his ankle. I followed its trail realizing it was some strange tendril made completely of water and its source was coming from Tallulah and her Spirit Caster. She pulled him down with it and slammed him into the ground, dragging him through all the rubble.

He quickly shot a blast from his hand to cut the tendril in half so he finally had a chance to stand on his own two feet. Though just from that single team combo alone he already looked bloody and beaten.

"The three of them are all so powerful," I commended.

"Yes," Céleste agreed. ***"Sage and Tallulah are masters when it comes to wielding their Spirit Casters. They both use their Rēa as efficiently as possible and could probably beat anyone who comes from your world in battle."***

"What about Reshma?" Crystal asked. "She seems just as efficient."

"As a fighter, yes. As a Shēna, no. Her Rēa has always been on the lower side. Luckily it's not something she relies on. She leans more towards her Zubarian heritage in times like this."

"Wait, she's a Shēna *and* a Zubarian? No wonder she's so strong."

That made Crystal pay a bit more attention to the fight.

"There's only two ways this can go!" Reshma shouted to Morpheus. "Either give up now, or die!"

"I've come too far to give up now!" he shouted back. "And there's no way I'm dying here! I've still got a couple of tricks up my sleeve!"

"Have it your way," she said while turning around to face Sage and Tallulah. "You two can finish him off, right?"

"Yeah," Tallulah answered. "You just focus on getting Aleron to safety so we don't end up killing him too."

Reshma nodded her head and ran towards him while Tallulah sat down on the ground as if she were about to meditate.

"Do you think you can keep him busy long enough to give me time to end this in one attack?" Tallulah asked.

"I don't know," Sage yawned. "I just made a full meal before this, so I'm still a little tired."

Tallulah reached into her pocket and tossed a pill at him. He caught it and gave her a grin.

"Yeah, now we're talking," he said before swallowing it whole. Flames burst from his body and even though we weren't physically there, I could still feel his heat.

"Woah, what did he just eat?" Crystal gasped.

"A gray pill," Céleste answered. **"Whoever consumes one, has all of their Rēa fully replenished. Sage is now back at his full strength."**

"He didn't even say a spell before unleashing his flames," I added. "He's skilled."

"Oh, is that what it looks like to you?" Céleste questioned. **"That's not his flames. That's just the physical manifestation of his Rēa."**

Those words made me silent. To be able to transform your own Rēa into something that's actually physical or even *tangible* is a feat that not many could even dream of. The only person who I knew of that could do something like that was my father. And somehow this boy was doing it without even trying.

Flames covered the entire battlefield forcing Morpheus to fly up from off the ground while Tallulah simply placed a protective bubble over herself so as to not get burnt. She was leaving this to the young boy.

Sage blasted off into the air and grabbed Morpheus, taking him higher than he intended and shouted, ***"Ékrixi!"***

A massive explosion lit up the sky and forced Morpheus to fall like a shooting star into the fire. But that didn't stop Sage's attack.

"Pyrini Vrochí!"

He once again swiped his Spirit Caster but this time small balls of fire came raining down making it so that no place was safe for Morpheus to go. All he could do was take the flames from the earth and the sky.

And if that wasn't enough, now there was another attack heading right towards him. Water rushed like a geyser from the sky past Sage and landed right on Morpheus with the force of a thousand waves. The water surged out and flooded the entire area, extinguishing the flames yet still somehow keeping its heat leaving the water at a boiling point. And maybe even putting Morpheus out of his misery. This was Tallulah's spell and I could now see why she needed time to prepare it.

"I can't believe they actually got him," Crystal gasped. "I couldn't even begin to guess the power that those two were hiding."

Céleste didn't respond to her. She just stayed silent and watched as if the battle wasn't over yet and that gave me a bad feeling.

Tallulah stood atop the water just like Delta did when we fought off those pirates and stared down into it.

"Is he dead?" Sage asked while hovering down closer to her.

"No, not yet," she squinted as if she could see him under the boiling lake. "He's a resilient one. But I don't imagine him lasting more than a minute down there. But even *that* would be giving him too much credit."

Suddenly, to her surprise, the water started rushing, making her stumble on its surface. She jumped away as a whirlpool was created in the center of the flooded field.

"I'm guessing this isn't you?" Sage shouted over the rushing water.

"Unfortunately, no! This guy really *did* have another trick up his sleeve! We'll have to find another way to beat him!"

Soon the water rose and dispersed until it turned to nothing but steam as if it disappeared into thin air. The only thing left standing on the battlefield was Morpheus. But not as we once knew him. His skin was even more pale than before. Like that of a ghoulish creature. His hair had turned completely white and grew down to his lower back. The whites of his eyes had darkened and his pupils stayed red. And finally two horns grew from each side of his head.

My heart sank watching his transformation. It was the same form that my father went into to fight Crystal and her friends. And it was the same form that *I* went into, forcing me to destroy my own city. I looked over at Crystal and she was staring at me with an intense look. She remembered this form all too well. I'm pretty sure I broke her arm with it.

"What is that thing?" asked Sage.

"Anástasi," Tallulah answered. "It's a transformation that boosts the user's strength, speed and magical abilities. Be on guard, this fight won't be easy."

"Oh so you know of this form?" Morpheus's voice echoed the same way my father's voice echoed when he too entered that form. As if they were now something more than human. "I didn't want to use this so soon but you two were able to push me to my limits. I didn't plan for any of you to be this strong. You should take pride in your abilities. I hope that puts you at ease for your deaths." He released a terrifying aura that made Crystal and I shutter and even made Sage and Tallulah take a few steps back. "Come at me!"

Sage didn't hesitate to take on the challenge. He went blasting off towards Morpheus with his flames ready to attack. But he was just playing into his hand.

"Sage, wait!" Tallulah shouted but it was in vain.

Within the blink of an eye Morpheus flew past Sage and aimed his sights towards Tallulah. Her guard was down and no one was ready for him. With immense speed and strength he tore his hands right through her chest and quickly ripped her heart out. She didn't even have enough time to scream.

Sage turned around only having enough time to show a single reaction.

"Tallulah!" he screamed, immediately turning around to try and save the already lost life, but before he could fully turn Morpheus already used his unnatural speed to get back behind Sage, grab him by his head and snap his neck out of place, making his body immediately go limp. The worst part of it all was that he did it all with a smile on his face.

"No," Crystal trembled. "This is ... This is wrong! Why aren't we down there? Why are you just sitting there and letting this happen?" she screamed. "How many bodies does he have to pile on your doorstep before you decide to take action?"

Céleste didn't look at Crystal. She just glared at Morpheus with eyes that began to glow, making Crystal and I take a step away from her. And without ever saying a single word, she simply vanished in thin air, taking the image of the battlefield with her.

"What happened?" Crystal asked, looking around in every direction. "Where'd she go?"

"Isn't it obvious?" I told her. "She's finally taking your advice."

CHAPTER THIRTY-THREE
ARACHNE

"**A**re you two alright?" Morpheus shouted at us.

Wren, Kian and I were atop one of the towers after the battlefield got bombarded by fire. I looked down at Kian and he looked shell shocked. It wasn't from the attacks but from Morpheus. Not only because his appearance was that of a monster but from the murder he just now witnessed. It was a child not too much older than Kian himself. That child may have been anything but defenseless but he was too young to have such a sudden fate.

"Yeah we're fine!" I shouted back.

"Good. Then make your way down here. We're not done here, and I don't want to waste any more time on these pawns. We need to find our way to the Queen as quickly as possible."

Then as if from thin air someone, or rather *something* appeared right behind him. Its body was human and somewhat feminine but its skin, if you could call it that, was like a void filled with small astral lights. This being was unlike anything I had ever seen before.

"There's no need," the entity said to Morpheus in a similar echoey tone.

Morpheus looked back at them and for the first time today he actually looked startled.

"What? No witty remarks? Are you surprised that you're actually in my presence? Your intentions were to gain my attention, was it not? What was so important for you to say that it was worth slaughtering my servants over?" It questioned him.

He looked back at me and did a quick nod. That was his signal. This thing ... it was the god we had to usurp. And it was time to enact the final stage of our plan.

He then looked back at her and asked, "Céleste I presume?"

She didn't answer. It was obvious who she was and the heat that emanated from her eyes showed just how much she didn't care for his pointless chitchat. She just sat there waiting for him to answer her question.

So he finally answered, "I'm here to avenge my mother; your own sister for your betrayal."

"So, it's true. She really did have a child. I didn't want to believe it, but I can feel her spirit flowing within you. Since you're her offspring I'll give you one last ultimatum. Surrender yourself or die."

"Oh please," he scoffed. "We both know you don't have any intention of letting me leave this place alive."

She took a deep breath and gave him a dry chuckle. ***"I guess you're right."*** She disappeared and reappeared inches from his face faster than he could react and much faster than I could comprehend. ***"Your death is inevitable."***

She quickly placed her hand on his stomach and shot a blast that sent him flying to the bottom of the tower that we were standing on, making us stumble from the crash. Before the smoke could clear from the impact, Morpheus shot his own beam at her forcing her to once again vanish out of its path.

Once the smoke cleared I could see that he was shooting the beam from his mouth. He turned his head to the side to hit her but she flew up out of its range and made her way towards him. He tried tracking her, destroying other towers in the process, but missed her completely. She flew circles around his beam and vanished to other points on the battlefield right before it could make contact with her.

She was distracted with Morpheus, so this was my chance to set up the trap.

"Kian, stay here," I told him before jumping off the tower with Wren still in my arms. I ran her to the middle of the battlefield and placed her on the ground in a spot with minimal rubble. I then swung off my backpack and took two separate items out. A piece of parchment that had the same ruins as the ones carved into the wall of the ice temple, and a bag of blue powder.

I poured the powder on the ground around Wren, trying to copy the symbols on the paper as closely as possible, enclosing an image of the sun, moon and stars.

I looked back at the battle and saw the goddess cut right through Morpheus's energy beam with her hand, going through it like rushing water. To stop the beam, she slammed her hand over his mouth and smashed his head back into the wall over and over again while saying, ***"Did you really think that you'd actually be able to dethrone me? I'm a god and you're nothing but a spoiled brat! Before I'm done with you, I'm going to make you pray for your own death. And when I feel up to it, I'll answer that prayer!"***

He pointed his finger at her to let out another blast, but she grabbed him by the wrist and pushed it aside before it could hit her. Then she continued slamming his head against the stone wall breaking off chunks of it with every throw. If he weren't using *anástasi* then his head would have been nothing but a bloody paste by now. He obviously stood no chance on his own and wasn't going to be able to lead her into the trap himself.

I went back into the bag and took out the final item needed for the spell. A Phoenix feather, courtesy of Flint. Now all I needed to do was get her attention.

I took my Spirit Caster out, pointed it at Céleste and shouted, ***"Bála Oxéos!"***

A green ball of ooze spilled from it and hit her right in the back forcing the goddess to drop Morpheus to the ground and turn her attention towards me. The poison was dripping down her body, but to my surprise, she barely even reacted to it. If any normal person, or even Shēna for that matter were to be hit by that, then their skin would burn off and maybe even melt through their bones if they had enough on them. But she wasn't taking any damage at all.

"What was that supposed to do? Did you think that would hurt me?" she squinted at me.

I put away my wand and took out the piece of parchment with the feather still in my other hand and spoke the ancient incantation while backing away.

"Come, let me covet
Now Let me devour your soul
Let me take from you."

"It doesn't matter what spell you use, girl," she warned me while slowly strolling after me. *"Our powers are of two completely different dimensions. Nothing you do will have any effect on me."*

I continued anyway.

"Now give it to me
Your mind, your body, your soul
I want it all now."

She raised her hand towards me, forming an energy blast that could probably wipe me out in an instant and said, *"I told you it's pointless. Stand down now or I'll erase you."*

I couldn't stop now. We've come too far to give up. We were far past the point of no return. So the threat of oblivion was outweighed by the gift of godhood.

"Let me hear you scream!

I want to hear you suffer
In the name of God!"

"Have it your way," she scoffed, readying to blast away. But she stopped. Something caught her eye. She looked down and saw my powder on the ground along with Wren's body. She was finally in my trap and the conditions had been met!

"What is this?" she asked, completely oblivious to my next move.

I answered with a single word. ***"Stachyologó."***

Blue flames erupted from the powder as Wren started to float in the air high above us.

The goddess tried to escape the circle but couldn't. Even her vanishing technique didn't work. It was like she was being stopped by an invisible wall.

Morpheus was finally able to pull himself back to his feet while laughing with more glee and energy then I had ever seen from him.

"What is this?" she shouted at him.

"Think of it as a little gift from your sister," he answered with a mischievous smirk.

Her eyes widened as she realized the true danger of her situation. ***"Release me!"*** she commended.

"In time. After you give me exactly what I want."

He then took out a Phoenix feather of his own and pointed it in our direction. In that same moment Wren was thrusted awake. Electricity shot from her body causing her to once again scream in complete and utter agony. The electricity shot right through the god's body, stopping her movements and forcing her to scream right along with the child. It didn't take long for the electricity to reach Morpheus and his feather. Once it connected, the transmutation began.

The astral skin that covered Céleste's body started to peel off like wood shavings and floated onto Morpheus, connecting to his skin instead. He was taking everything from her. All of her power and then some.

Once the process was finished, she fell straight to the ground on her hands and knees. Her skin was dark. No longer as dark as the night sky but of mahogany. And her hair was no longer a storm. It was just curly. And now her features were more defined so I could see her naked body. She looked more human now.

"What— what did you do to me?" she asked with a flat voice.

Morpheus walked right over to us looking completely different. His skin looked just like hers before. It was dark purple with a cluster of stars spiraling around him. The only difference is that he still kept his horns from *anástasi.* And now he had a floating halo behind his head that looked almost like a crown.

"I took you down a peg," he finally answered. ***"Welcome to mortality."***

My heart skipped a beat. He was beautiful. He was powerful. He was everything that a normal man could never be. He was a god.

CHAPTER THIRTY-FOUR
KIRA

Once again Crystal was pacing back and forth while I sat on the throne steps. But this time, not only were we completely in the dark about our situation, but we were also alone. That was something that Crystal couldn't stand for.

"I'm leaving," she told me.

"You shouldn't," I told her back.

"And why's that?"

"Because he was able to beat everyone back home. Delta, Ranne and all your friends ... everyone might be ..." it was hard for me to continue. I didn't want to think the worst. "Look if you go out there now and face him, you'll probably die."

She looked with furious eyes and walked up to me until she was right above me.

"That's the same thing I told myself the night you killed my parents. I'm *not* making that mistake again."

She then turned around to make her way out of the room, leaving me to only feel worse about my past actions. Just when I thought there was a chance she might've forgiven me, she just confirmed that things between us will never change. My *past* will never change. I can't believe that I thought just because I took an arrow for her then that would somehow redeem me. I won't get redemption until I end up just like the rest of my victims. Dead and forgotten. And if that was my fate against Morpheus then so be it.

"Crystal, wait," I stopped her from going through the door. She looked at me with an annoyed look but I hoped that would change with my next words. "I'm coming with you."

I couldn't see her next reaction because before another word could be spoken something monstrous ... something that I could barely even make out suddenly appeared right in front of me and grabbed me by my neck. Not even a second later my surroundings changed, and we were outside. The monster threw me to the ground giving me only a moment to understand what was happening.

I looked around and realized that I was on the battlefield. To my left was a naked woman on her hands and knees. Next to her I saw Wren on the ground with tears streaming down her face. Her breath was heavy as steam emanated from her body. I couldn't even begin to imagine what pain she had gone through.

Standing over her was Arachne. I wasn't sure if she was the one who hurt her. What would have even been the reason?

I looked to my right, and to my complete surprise I saw the last person I'd expect to see here.

"Kian?" I muttered before starting to crawl to him. "Kian, are you ok?"

I was stopped by a thin beam of dark energy that shot in between us. I looked at the source and finally got a good look at the *monster* who captured me. He looked just like Céleste but with a purple glow. He had horns and black eyes with a floating ring atop his head. Although he didn't look much like him anymore, I could still tell this thing was Morpheus. Although now he was anything but human.

"He's fine," he told me in a voice that was even more terrifying than before. ***"And he doesn't need your help."***

"Why is he here?" I asked him. "He's got nothing to do with this!"

Morpheus walked to a nearby rock that was broken from the rubble and took a seat. ***"Nothing to do with this?"*** he chuckled. ***"He's half the reason I'm here."***

"What do you mean by that?" I asked him before looking at Kian. "What's he talking about?"

Kian was silent. He looked to Morpheus as if he needed permission from him to answer.

"Go ahead, Brother." he gestured forward. ***"She's going to die today regardless. She has a right to know why."***

*Brother? This entire time he was Morpheus's **brother**?* It was then that I realized Kian was playing me the entire time.

Kian looked back at me and said, "I'm here because I want revenge. I want to watch you suffer for what you did to our mother."

I was taken aback by his new demeanor. But even more so towards his accusation.

"What *I* did?" I questioned.

"Don't play dumb with me! I saw you flying in the sky that day, destroying and killing everything and everyone in your path. Including my home. And *our* own mother."

"Kian" I clenched, "I'm sorry. I wasn't in control. And Morpheus," I turned to him. "I hated you but I would have never purposely gone after your mother. You should know that much."

"My mother?" Morpheus questioned as if he was barely paying attention. ***"Oh right, Melany. She was a close friend, but our bond stops there. She wasn't my mother."***

"But ... Kian just said *'our'* mother."

Kian looked at me with watery eyes and balled fist. "She was *your* mother too you idiot!"

"W-what are you talking about? My mother's dead!"

"Well now she is." Morpheus chuckled.

I got up to my feet and stormed my way towards him while yelling, "Enough of these games!"

Morpheus raised his Rēa, forcing everyone to the ground. Even Arachne. His energy was higher than anything I had ever felt in my life. It completely dwarfed my father's, and it felt like I was being crushed under its weight.

"Kian," Morpheus began to say, ***"you shouldn't be so harsh on her. You need to keep in mind that she thought her mother died the day you were born."***

"Morpheus ..." it was hard for me to breathe. "Don't look at him ... Look at me ... Tell me everything you *think* I don't know."

"Well, there's a lot you don't know, Kira," he chuckled once more. *"I suppose a good place to start is our heritage. First off, you Kian and I all shared the same father, Cole Black. I however don't share the same mother as the two of you."*

"You're lying!"

"He's telling the truth," the naked woman beside me said. I wasn't sure at first but after hearing her voice I was positive. It was Céleste. She continued saying, "Just like I sensed Cole Black's blood within you, I sensed the same as with them."

"But how? I don't understand ..."

"You were told that your mother died in childbirth, right?" Morpheus started to explain. *"Well, that wasn't true. Our father was the one who arranged that 'death'.*

"But she was his wife ... My mother! Why would he want to kill her?"

Morpheus grabbed a few pebbles from off the floor and started to levitate them above his hand as if he was still getting used to his new power. *"Because she hated him. And she hated you for becoming just like him. So, she wanted out. She tried to leave and take Kian with her. But our father didn't like that one bit. So I had to save her and help her fake her death.*

"That's bullshit! Why would you of all people help her?"

"Because just like you, I hated that man," He explained while crushing the rocks into powder. *"Undermining him in any way I could gave me a rush. It's why I had Arachne put that cancer in him."*

"You did *what?*" I shouted while trying to stand, but his overwhelming power made me crumble back to the floor. "You had a hand in killing my father?" I growled.

"As did you," he scoffed. **"You should honestly be thanking me. I freed you for a short time."**

"I don't understand. None of this makes any sense. You hurt Delta. You hurt Ranne. You helped kill my father and took away my mother. And you followed me all the way here to steal the power of a god? For what? To spite me? What was any of this for? Why have you been trying to torment me my entire life? What's so special about me that forced you to hate me from the moment you laid eyes on me?"

"There's nothing special about you Kira. I used to think there was. I wondered why our father chose you. He knew about me ya know. I doubt that he knew Kian was alive and he definitely didn't know I was his forgotten son after all this time that I worked for him. But he knew he got my mother pregnant. Yet he still cast me and my mother away. He chose you. I always wondered why. But after watching you guys for years I've come to the conclusion that maybe it was because you were the perfect punching bag. You're weak. Easy to manipulate. Worthless. Everything I'm not. So to answer your question, no Kira, there isn't anything special about you. You're just another pawn in a much bigger game."

He then gestured his hand over to Céleste and said, *"Speaking of which, have you met Céleste? She's my aunt. My mother's sister to be exact. And yet another person to cast her away. The first actually.*

"Your mother was dangerous!" Céleste argued. "She was going to destroy all of humanity as you know it!"

"So you chose humans over your own family? It's ironic that now you're nothing more than a human. And I won't be on your side either. You're going to die alongside Kira. But don't worry," he finally stood up from his rock, seemingly done without any more explanations, *"since we're all family I'll make it quick and painless."*

He thought he already won. His guard was down. This meant that I only had one shot at this.

I pulled out my new Spirit Caster and shouted, "*Désmi Thanátou!*" I expected a thin beam of energy to shoot out and pierce him right through his skull, but nothing happened.

Morpheus looked surprised for only a moment before regaining his composure and saying, *"I didn't realize you got a hold of a new Spirit Caster. But it seems you have no idea how to use it."*

He raised his hand forming a destructive ball of energy in front of it and pointed it right at me.

"Looks like our dad was right. You're nothing but a disappointment."

Before he could shoot off the blast another spell was let off.

"Cheimoniátiki Kataigída!"

A burst of icy wind and snow erupted across the battlefield, hurling us all backwards, everyone except Morpheus that is. He remained unfazed, casually turning his attention away from me to peer into the distance, searching for the source of the spell.

"Ahh, it seems that Ms. Winters has finally decided to join the party."

Crystal's spell was the perfect cover to escape. I immediately got up and ran straight to Wren, picking her up and yelling to Céleste, "We need to move, *now*!"

Morpheus turned his attention back to me and said, **"You're not going anywhere."**

He raised his hand back towards me, but before he could attack, Crystal grabbed his wrist and swung her Spirit Caster against his chest as if it were a blade while yelling, **"Cheimerinó Fengári!"**

Ice rushed out and froze the upper half of his body.

Crystal turned back to us while he was frozen and yelled, "Get back to the portal! We need to get out of this dimension right now!"

Morpheus broke out of the ice but not unscathed. He had a giant gash on his chest where she swiped her Spirit Caster. I didn't think a creature as powerful as him could even take damage, but Crystal proved that he can be wounded. He can be *killed*.

He looked at her with his signature mischievous grin and said, **"Impressive. I didn't see you coming and you were actually** *able to damage me. My hunch about you was right. You're not like the others. I want to see your limits."*

able to damage me. My hunch about you was right. You're not like the others. I want to see your limits."

CHAPTER THIRTY-FIVE
CRYSTAL

Morpheus shot a ball of energy at me, causing me to blast away, hitting the floor hard. Oddly enough it didn't hurt as bad as I thought it would. Felt more like a firm push rather than an actual death beam. My new armor must've protected me from the blast because there wasn't a single tear in the fabric.

Before I could get back up, Morpheus jumped up high into the air with the full intention of hitting me with another attack. He wrapped energy around his fist and tried to punch me, but I rolled out of the way before he could hit me. Unfortunately, it caused a wide burst of energy to once again push me a large distance away, but this time I landed on my feet.

He continued his pursuit by flying towards me at full speed, but before he could reach me, I shouted the spell, ***"Toícho Ton Thrafsmáton!"***

It created a wall of ice shards that was meant to pierce him, but he came to a grinding halt right before hitting it. He then placed his hand on the ice, and without saying any spell he simply shattered it with his own Rēa, but I was ready for that.

I had already set up my ice spear and shouted, *"To Pagáki Ekteínetai!"*

The spear extended and almost pierced through him, but he disappeared and reappeared right behind me before I could hit.

"Your reaction speed has improved by a large margin," he praised. *"And you're able to sustain more damage than I expected."*

I retracted my ice and saw blood on the tip. I hit him. He wasn't using any illusions. Somehow this time he had actually gained the ability to teleport. I turned around to look at him. He looked similar to how Céleste looked, but he was using *Anástasi.* The combination made something unworldly.

"You *also* seem to have gone through a few changes since the last time we met," I remarked. "Care to fill me in since you love running your mouth?"

Although I genuinely was curious on how someone like him could gain such a godly amount of power in such a short amount of time, my main goal was to stall him so that Kira could get Wren as far away from him as possible. And what better way for that to happen than it being from his own ego.

"Forgive me, it didn't occur to me that maybe my new state of being might be jarring to you," he apologized. *"The last time you saw me, I only had the Illusion Spirit Caster in my possession. But now I have the power of the Darkness Spirit Caster and the astral energy of Space flowing through*

my veins. At this moment, I'm at a completely different level of power that someone like you could never comprehend."

"How the hell did you pull something like that off?"

"Oh, I have your sister to thank for that," he grinned.

I quickly placed my spear to his neck and asked, "Why did you take her? And what did you do to her?"

"In order to get this new power, I needed a few sacrifices. Tal and Torra fulfilled their purpose, but Wren exceeded my expectations."

"Sacrifices?" I shuddered. "Alizeh's father... and Rai's grand-mother... you *killed* them?

"I used their souls to lay the foundation for my new power. But your sister, she's special. Perhaps even more special than you. She's the only survivor of the ritual. In fact, she had enough Rēa for me to siphon in order to steal the powers of a god. I would've needed hundreds of average souls to pull that off and somehow, she's still alive. So her usefulness to me hasn't reached its limit."

"I won't let you touch her again!" I roared.

"That's not your call," he smirked.

I thrusted my spear towards his neck, but he disappeared again before I could make contact. I looked around and he was nowhere to be seen. It only took him a few moments to return with a familiar dark-skinned woman, Kira and worst of all, Wren.

He then powered up his Rēa and with nothing but his own spiritual power, he was able to completely disperse my storm, making the sky clear and the wind silent.

"Alright, I believe I've given everyone the answers they were looking for. Is everyone satisfied? Good. Now you can all die with no regrets."

"You're delusional if you think I'm going down without a fight," I said as I raised my spear.

"I wouldn't expect anything less from you, Crystal."

He took a few steps towards me but was stopped in his tracks from a blast that shot down at him from the sky. We all looked up and saw some kind of flying vessel, hovering in the sky while lowering itself over to us. It didn't stop its assault on Morpheus, and for a moment it was successful at holding him at bay.

Once the vessel opened up, dozens of soldiers flooded out to attack Morpheus but all that meant was that they were walking into their death. One by one he took them all down making his way closer to us. I was prepared to join in on their fight, but I was stopped by someone else on the vessel.

"All of you, get on the ship, now!"

I looked back and saw Abraham gesturing to us.

The dark-skinned lady ran to the ship and Kira followed behind but stopped when she realized I wasn't right behind her.

"Crystal, what are you waiting for?" Kira shouted at me. "We have to go!"

"I can take him."

"No, you can't!"

"I wanna try."

"You'll die trying!" Abraham shouted over us. "We need to re-group and live to fight another day!

"But—"

"Crystal, think about your sister," Kira reminded me. "If you die here then who's going to take care of her? *Me*?"

Now that was something I couldn't let happen. I finally turned around and followed them to the ship, jumping on as it started to hover away from the floating island.

I looked around on the ship and saw Aleron laying off to the side while being healed by Ziva and Haoma while Reshma was steering the magical vessel itself. Abraham was tending to the dark-skinned cloaked woman.

I went close to Kira and asked, "Who is that?"

"Queen Céleste unfortunately."

I took a double take before Kira continued, "I was honestly just as confused as you are now, but I'm assuming that this is what happens when a god's power is stolen. They turn out just like us."

So, Morpheus wasn't lying. He really did steal her power, turn-ing her into nothing in comparison. I wondered how big of a threat he truly was in that state.

Kira looked over to Reshma and asked, "Where are we going?"

"Far away from here. Like Abraham said, we need to regroup and find another way to beat that monster."

Just then Wren's cough cut right through the conversation.

"She's waking up," Kira told me.

"Give her to me," I insisted.

I took her and held her in my arms as she opened her blood shot eyes. It was almost unsettling until they immediately started to water.

"Crystal, is that you?" Wren choked.

"Yes Wren," I smiled, "It's me."

Wren clenched onto me, "Why... Why did you leave me?"

My smile faded away from the hurt in her voice.

"Why did you let them take me? Why didn't you take me with you?" she cried.

"Wren," my voice cracked, "I'm sorry..."

"Everything still hurts!" she screamed through her sobs. "They wouldn't stop hurting me! Where were you? You promised you'd come back!"

Her words made me realize that I was consumed so much by revenge that I forgot my first ever rule. That rule being to fight to protect my family. My quest for vengeance was selfish, and I never stopped to consider how it would affect the only family I had left. If I never went on this forsaken quest for revenge then Wren would have never been in any danger.

I squeezed her and cried, "I'm sorry that I couldn't save you in time. But I'm here now. And I'm never leaving you *ever* again. We're gonna go home and I'll make sure no one ever hurts you again."

Wren tried to control her breathing and sniffled, "Do you promise?"

I put my face close to rub my nose against hers, forcing her to actually crack a stressed smile.

"I promise."

I wish I could've held onto that moment but something sinister put a chill down my spine. Everyone glared at me... or rather past me. Even Wren as she was in my arms. She stopped breathing once she saw the face of the man who had tortured her.

"I thought I already told you, that girl is too valuable for me to let her go."

I looked back and saw that Morpheus had suddenly appeared in the ship from his new teleportation ability.

I was frozen in his presence. I wasn't ready for him as he casually walked closer to me. I clenched onto Wren but she clenched onto me even tighter.

Aleron used all his strength to get up and was the first one to attack like a true warrior. But it was fruitless. Morpheus simply scoffed and literally swatted him away like a bug, and without even touching him, Aleron flew against the wall of the ship breaking right through it and flying out, leaving a gaping hole that was trying to suck the rest of us out along with him. We all tried to keep our balance and as long as we could do that then the rest of us would be safe. That was easier said than done.

Reshma rushed out of her seat to take vengeance for her lover. But Morpheus did the same with her, except this time he threw her into the controls forcing the ship to spiral out of control. We all fell and for one moment I lost my grip on Wren. She rolled and tumbled to the shattered wall, and I tried to catch her but tripped, allowing her to fly right off the vessel.

"Wren!" I screamed, not hesitating for even a moment to go after her.

Kira tried to reach out to me, calling my name for me to stop but I ignored her and jumped off the ship in a free fall.

This wasn't my first time dealing with a situation like this. I had survived my fall in Ebony and I'd do it again here. I just needed to catch her and make another slide made of ice for us to survive.

But she was too far away already. I straightened my body to dive towards her and made it close. Almost close enough to grab her until there was a blue flash of light in front of me. Once again Morpheus had teleported to me and sucker punched me right in my face making me fly off from my original trajectory. And when I was completely out of reach, he grabbed Wren and teleported away. Though, not before I heard her screaming my name. That would be the last time.

I was so close. I had her in my grasp and after promising that I'd keep her safe, promising that I'd never let anyone touch her again ... I failed. She was gone to an unknown fate that I couldn't stop. I wanted to scream. I wanted to kill Morpheus more than I ever wanted to kill Kira or anyone else for that matter. But I couldn't. I fell right down to the sand with an explosive impact that completely took me out.

CHAPTER THIRTY-SIX
ARACHNE

Kian and I were left to sit and look across the sea of bodies. The battlefield was desolate and vast but Kian put all of his attention into one body. The young boy that fought against Morpheus and got his neck snapped. Seeing his older brother kill someone so young must've been shocking to him. Hell, it was shocking to me. But the kid was in the way of our plans and Morpheus already told me once that he didn't care who it was that would get in his way. They'd die all the same.

Morpheus finally reappeared in front of me while holding Wren close to him. She jumped out of his arms trying to get away, but he snatched her by her wrist, stopping her. That didn't stop her from using all her strength to try and break free. She bit and clawed at him while screaming, well past the verge of tears.

"You're starting to annoy me," Morpheus told her. *"Keep it up and I'll break your arm. Hell, I'll rip it off if I have to. It's not like you'll need it for what I have planned for you."*

That threat seemed to only make her scream even more. Poor kid just didn't know how to shut up and now she was going to suffer for it.

"Fine, have it your way."

Once he tightened his grip it looked like he was actually going to go through with it until Kian grabbed him by the same arm, stopping him from going any further. Kian looked at him with an intense glare.

"What is it?" Morpheus asked, cocking his head to the side.

"You've hurt a lot of people today. And you've killed a lot too. I don't like it, but everyone you've hurt was in the way of our plans. But this girl hasn't done anything. All you've done is take from her. She's innocent, and I don't think she deserves any more pain."

Morpheus glared at the boy, but Kian glared right back. This child was literally challenging god. And luckily, he had his favor. Morpheus let go of Wren causing her to fall down to the ground in disbelief.

Kian crouched down to console her and said, "Don't worry, I'm not gonna let him hurt you anymore."

"As long as you can keep her in line then I won't have to," Morpheus cut in. **"She's your responsibility from now on."**

To Kian it must've seemed like he saved a life. But I could tell that Morpheus had just taken the chance to give Kian a new pet.

Morpheus started to walk away, forcing me to ask, "Where are you going?"

"Our work here isn't done yet," Morpheus answered. ***"We still have plenty of loose ends to tie up. The power dynamic has shifted, and this world needs to know who its new ruler is. Now come. Let's show them."***

Kian reached his hand out to Wren and she reluctantly held on to it and followed. She should feel honored. She was getting front row seats to a new era. She was going to watch us become gods.

CHAPTER THIRTY-SEVEN
ANA

I woke up from the wet snow grazing my face. It was snowing. My chest was in pain from that stab wound so sitting up felt like torture. Luckily someone had already put bandages over the open bloody wound. But I didn't understand why they'd take me outside of all places.

I looked around to see more people in a similar position as me, if not worse. And others frantically running around to aid them.Cara ran up to me with more bandages along with needles and threads before getting down on one knee.

"Good," she huffed. "You're awake. Thought we lost you."

I didn't take my eyes off the carnage as I asked her, "Where are we?"

"The temple," she answered. "Or at least what's left of it."

I pushed past the pain to get back up on my feet to confirm her horrific claim. Everything was gone. The only thing left was rubble and the foundation that it was built upon. The aftermath of the attack made my home look like the ruins of a lost civilization.

"You shouldn't be standing," Cara suggested. "That wound's pretty deep."

I ignored the sentiment.

"Where's my mother?" I asked.

Cara took a moment to answer me before saying, "We haven't found her yet. But everyone's still searching."

I started to walk off prompting her to ask, "Where are you going?"

"That should be obvious," I told her. "I'm gonna go find her."

I walked past the bodies that were covered in a light blanket of snow. None of them were breathing. Some of them were even worse off. Their skin boiled off by poison and their limbs crushed by stone. It was a graveyard with no undertaker.

I knew these men and women. All friends and allies. But there was one body that I had never seen. He was faced down on the floor and he was breathing. I knelt down to turn him around to get a better look and sure enough I had no idea who this blonde-haired child was. Even more interesting was the Spirit Caster he was clenching.

I looked around until something caught my eye. Something, or rather *someone* more familiar. I bolted towards the bloodied body to see if they were still alive. The small girl was beaten more than I'd ever seen from her before.

"Alizeh?" I shook her.

She didn't wake up. Why was she here? Why was she *dying*? What happened while I was out?

There was no time for me to figure out the answer to any of these questions. I picked her up, tossed her over my shoulder and did the same with the other boy. I had a feeling that these two had the answers I needed so letting them die wasn't an option.

CHAPTER THIRTY-EIGHT
KIRA

◯

I opened my eyes to see a slightly familiar face. It was the same woman who took Crystal's *x-ray*. Ziva's assistant.

"Oh, thank Céleste!" Haoma beamed. "You're awake."

I quickly sat up and looked around and asked, "Where's Crystal?"

"We haven't found her body yet," she answered solemnly.

Getting up to my feet was a hassle. I was too dizzy to stand on my own, so I leaned on the wall of the broken ship, trying to avoid the sparks that spilled from their malfunctioning devices.

I held my head for a moment, trying to shake my fatigue away just to see blood covering my hand from the wound on my temple.

"You talk as if she's already dead." I finally responded.

"She jumped off the hovercraft while we were still in the sky," she pointed out.

"She's survived worse," I told her before walking off the ruined ship.

It was a familiar sight. The sand dunes that I traversed every time I used *Grigoro Taxidi*. Except this time there wasn't a dark shroud impeding my vision like a vague nightmare.

Everyone surrounded Céleste as she laid in the sand. I quickly got close to see that Ziva was busy healing her bloody leg.

Once Abraham looked back and noticed me, he said, "Good, you're alive."

"What happened to her?" I asked as I got to his side.

"A piece of shrapnel tore through her leg during the crash. But it's a wound that Ziva can handle so she'll survive."

I continued to look down at the fallen god. It was jarring to see that just an hour ago she was the strongest being in the universe. Now she's more fragile than even me.

Reshma turned away from the group and started to walk off into the void.

"I'm leaving," she told everyone.

"Where are you going?" Abraham asked.

"To find my husband, obviously."

"You need to wait until Céleste is back on her feet."

"She'll live," Reshma scoffed while turning back to him. "And you're capable enough to protect her on your own."

"That's not the point," he said in a stern tone as he walked up to face her, even though she towered over him. "We need to stick together. Anything could be lurking down here, and we need to create a solid plan so we can decide our next move."

Reshma's eyes beamed red. But not in a combative way. It seemed almost unintentional. Like she was filled with so much rage that she desperately tried to hold back.

"Ziva never cured him of that poison," she finally said. "And I don't know how much time he has. If I don't find him now, then he'll die."

A screech cut through their argument. We all turned in different directions to see animal-like silhouettes closing in on us. Even though these creatures were all different shapes and sizes, they all seemed familiar as they got closer. These monsters looked just like the ones we had to fight in the underground sewers of Ebony.

"What are they?" I shuddered as I backed away towards the rest of the group.

"Husks," Abraham answered. "Mindless beast with a never-ending hunger."

"And they see *us* as prey," Reshma added.

I tightened my grip on my new wand. Not out of determination but fear. There were so many of them and I didn't know how to use a single spell. But I *had* to find a way to survive. I needed to find Crystal and get back home to Ranne. And even more importantly I needed to kill Morpheus for what he did to me. For what he did to *everyone*. For hurting *Ranne*. And I'm not dying until I see that through.

www.ingramcontent.com/pod-product-compliance
Lightning Source LLC
Chambersburg PA
CBHW032350310726
48973CB00007B/1943